A Christmas Kiss

Nicole followed Luc down a narrow side street. But she stopped short as a brilliant string of silvery Christmas lights suddenly blinked on over the doorway of the small café they were passing, instantly transforming an ordinary doorway into a tableau worthy of the fanciest of the department stores out on the broad Parisian avenues.

"Ooh, it's beautiful!" Nicole stopped short, gazing up at the display.

Luc stepped over and looped an arm around her shoulders, looking up as well. *"Mais oui,"* he said. "And look—another lovely view."

Nicole looked where he was pointing and realized that the Eiffel Tower had just come into view over the tops of the buildings. Gazing up at it, she experienced a weird moment of déjà vu. Then she realized she was recalling another time when she and Luc had suddenly come upon a spectacular view of La Tour Eiffel. That time had ended in an unexpected but incredible kiss . . .

She shivered and looked up at him, only to find his green eyes already gazing down at her. They locked eyes for a moment, neither of them moving a muscle even as cars and trucks rumbled past on the narrow street and pedestrians buried in their winter wear hurried past all around them.

"Ah, Nicole," Luc said, though it came out as more of a sigh. "*Ma chérie . . .*"

Without further ado, he turned her toward him and kissed her. Nicole's heart was pounding furiously. She knew she should push him away—wasn't this undoing all the good of their little chat earlier? But somehow, she couldn't seem to do it. She couldn't seem to *want* to do it.

French Kissmas

Cathy Hapka

speak
An Imprint of Penguin Group (USA) Inc.

SPEAK
Published by the Penguin Group
Penguin Group (USA) Inc.,
345 Hudson Street, New York, New York 10014, U.S.A.
Penguin Group (Canada), 90 Eglinton Avenue East, Suite 700, Toronto, Ontario, Canada M4P 2Y3
(a division of Pearson Penguin Canada Inc.)
Penguin Books Ltd, 80 Strand, London WC2R 0RL, England
Penguin Ireland, 25 St Stephen's Green, Dublin 2, Ireland
(a division of Penguin Books Ltd)
Penguin Group (Australia), 250 Camberwell Road, Camberwell, Victoria 3124, Australia
(a division of Pearson Australia Group Pty Ltd)
Penguin Books India Pvt Ltd, 11 Community Centre, Panchsheel Park,
New Delhi - 110 017, India
Penguin Group (NZ), 67 Apollo Drive, Rosedale, North Shore 0632,
New Zealand (a division of Pearson New Zealand Ltd)
Penguin Books (South Africa) (Pty) Ltd, 24 Sturdee Avenue, Rosebank, Johannesburg 2196,
South Africa

Registered Offices: Penguin Books Ltd, 80 Strand, London WC2R 0RL, England

Published by Speak, an imprint of Penguin Group (USA) Inc., 2008

1 3 5 7 9 10 8 6 4 2

CIP DATA IS AVAILABLE

SPEAK ISBN 978-0-14-241133-9

Printed in the United States of America

Arc de Triomphe
Eiffel Tower

Nicole's Paris

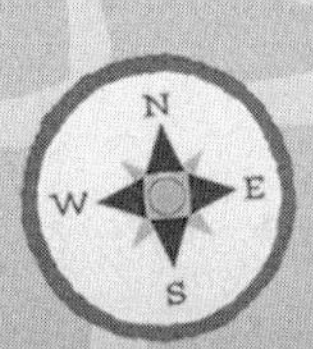

15 September

Dear S.A.S.S. alumnus,

It is our delight to inform you that S.A.S.S. will be adding a new program to its schedule next year. Because of the success of our worldwide study-abroad program—that success made possible by dedicated students like you!—we will be offering a three-week Wintermission program in select European cities for those who cannot make the time commitment to a full semester or summer program but still wish to take advantage of the wonderful opportunities for growth and learning provided by experiencing a new culture.

To help get the word out about this new program, we will be shooting a promotional video for our Web site. We hope to involve past and current students in the project, and would like to invite all S.A.S.S. alumni and current applicants to participate. Those interested must be available over the holidays in any of our shooting locations—Dublin, Paris, Munich, or Rome. Lodging (if needed) and a modest per diem will be provided. Please see the Web site for more information. We hope to see you again soon!

Sincerely,
The S.A.S.S. staff

French Kissmas

Chapter One

"Toiletries...check. Laundry stuff...check," Nicole Larson muttered.

She leaned over the bed and gave the contents of her backpack a firm shove, trying to gauge whether she had any realistic hope of closing the zipper. She was pretty sure she could do it—barely. Then she shot one more glance around the small room in the Venetian *pensione* that she had occupied for the past two weeks. It still looked a bit messy. The sheets were crumpled down at the ends of both twin beds. The tiny wastebasket was spilling over with tissues and other trash. Nicole's laptop and cell

phone, which would be the last things she packed away in her roomy shoulder bag, were perched atop the rickety table near the door along with her passport belt and a half-full bottle of San Pellegrino.

However, all other traces of Nicole had been removed from the room. The drawers of the old-fashioned upright bureau stood open and empty. Her paperback book, breath mints, and hairbrush had disappeared from the bedside table. But wait...what was that peeking out from under the bed...?

Nicole groaned. "Extra shoes...not check," she said, pushing a strand of blond hair out of her eyes and bending down to retrieve her sneakers from their hiding place. "Oh, man. How in the world am I supposed to fit *these* in here...?"

"Talking to yourself again?" a playful voice asked from the doorway.

Nicole glanced up as her best friend, Patrice Fiorelli, hurried into the room carrying a bag of snacks she'd just bought. Even though Patrice had been in Venice for almost five days, it still felt strange to see her familiar pixie-ish face and dancing brown eyes there among the exotic piazzas and canals. Strange, but nice. After the three-plus months Nicole had spent traveling around Europe by herself, it was wonderful to have familiar company, even if only for a week.

"Sort of," Nicole admitted. "I don't know why my stuff

won't fit back in my bags. I've only been in Venice for a couple of weeks—it's not like I got that much new stuff here!" She tossed the sneakers on top of her bloated backpack, then glanced at the smaller rolling suitcase that was already zipped and standing near the door, wondering if there was any space left in there. "I mean, sure, I noticed it was a *little* harder to get everything zipped up when I left Florence to come here, but really..."

"Well, you'd better either shove them in there somewhere or figure out how to wear them as a necklace," Patrice said, dragging her already-packed luggage out from under the bed. "The guy at the desk said the water taxi should be here in, um, *dieci minuti*. I think that means ten minutes." She giggled. "Or maybe it means 'go away, American girl, no taxi for you!' Who knows?"

Nicole grinned. She had missed Patrice's wacky sense of humor. Picking up her sneakers again, she shot a glance at her friend's bags. "You don't have any extra room in there, do you?" she asked hopefully.

Patrice playfully blocked her suitcases with her body. "No way!" she said. "You've been wearing those things for months—they stink. Anyway, you've got like five or six more months living out of those bags. You're in big trouble if you're running out of space already!"

"I know, I know." Nicole pulled a pair of jeans out of the backpack. She unfolded them and started rolling them into a sort of denim sausage, hoping that would save enough

space to squeeze the sneakers in. "I might have to go through all my stuff once we get to Paris and maybe send a few things home with you, if you don't mind."

"Sure." Patrice flopped down on her unmade bed and grinned up at Nicole. "Although I doubt you'll be in the mood for luggage sorting once you're reunited with Monsieur Hunky Hottie in Paris."

Nicole blushed, keeping her gaze firmly trained on the jeans in her hands. "Yeah, right," she muttered. "I told you, Luc and I are just friends now."

"Your mouth says *non non,*" Patrice said in a goofy French accent lifted straight from Pepé Le Pew. "But your eyes, zey say, *Oui! Oui!*"

"Very funny." Nicole rolled her eyes, but she couldn't help laughing. Patrice could always help her appreciate the goofy side of life. That was one of the reasons they got along so well. Nicole's more thoughtful temperament helped ground Patrice's natural giddiness a little, while Patrice was one of the few people who could coax Nicole into looking for the silver lining when she was feeling down. "Anyway, I wish more of my other Paris friends were going to be around so you could meet them. I can't believe the Smiths are living in Hong Kong now!" Nicole smiled at the thought of the American family she'd lived with in Paris during her semester abroad with the S.A.S.S. study-abroad program the previous year. The Smiths had four kids under the age of seven, which had made their apartment kind of chaotic at times, to say the least. But by the end of her stay, all six of them had felt like family to Nicole. "And it's just bad timing that you won't get to meet Marie and Renaud," she added.

"That's the older couple who lived downstairs from you, right?" Patrice asked, rolling over onto her stomach and resting her chin on her hand.

"Uh-huh."

Actually, the French couple—especially the wife, Marie—had been much more than downstairs neighbors to Nicole during her stay. Marie had helped her figure out some important things about herself and had been someone Nicole could always talk to even during her darkest moments in Paris. She had been terribly disappointed when she'd e-mailed Marie to tell her she would be coming back to Paris only to discover that Marie and Renaud would be visiting family in the south of France for the entire time Nicole was there.

"Well, those peeps sound cool and all." Patrice sat up and grinned, swinging her legs off the edge of the bed. "But I'm just glad Luc didn't decide to jaunt off to Hong Kong or anywhere else this Christmas. I'm totally looking forward to meeting your mysterious French *amour* at long last. I just hope I don't swoon and embarrass you when I lay eyes on his French gorgeousness."

Nicole smiled weakly. The closer the time came, the more she realized that she herself actually had mixed feelings about seeing Luc again. Part of her almost wished she wasn't getting the chance. True, he had played a huge role in making her semester abroad a very special time in her life; probably as much as Marie or the Smiths or anyone else. But she was sure it would seem weird to see him now, an entire year later. It would probably be easier if she could keep him firmly in the past where he belonged, a nice—albeit still a bit confusing—memory...

Don't be stupid, she chided herself, squeezing the rolled jeans in her hands. *It's not a big deal. Luc and I are friends now—that's all.*

On the surface at least, that was true. After she'd left Paris at the end of her semester, she and Luc had kept in touch via somewhat sporadic e-mails. They were pen pals. Friends.

So then why did she still shiver a little when she remembered the way he used to look at her, or that certain special kiss one evening in the shadow of the Eiffel Tower?

Patrice checked her watch. "Come on, we'd better get out there. We don't want to miss the train." She shivered and wrapped her arms around herself. "I can't believe I'm actually going to Paris!"

"I only wish you could stay there longer," Nicole said as she finally managed to wedge everything back into her bag and zip it up. Patrice had flown over to join her in Italy as soon as her college exams were finished. She'd wanted to make the trip longer than a week—as she'd said, it was a heck of a distance to go for seven measly days—but her family had insisted on having her home again in plenty of time for Christmas.

"Me, too. But hey, at least I'll get to experience one of those cramped little train sleeping compartments you keep complaining about in your e-mails."

Nicole laughed. She had to admit that the overnight train trips, like the one from Venice to Paris, were *not* her favorite parts of this adventure.

"Yeah; me, too," she teased playfully. "I call the bottom bunk!"

A moment later they were stepping out into the narrow, twisting street outside the *pensione*. The *vaporetto,* or water taxi, was already waiting for them at the edge of the nearest canal. As the operator loaded their bags onto the boat, Nicole breathed in the dank, slightly sour smell that hung over the city thanks to its network of canals, a scent that had already become familiar in just two weeks. The mementos she had bought and the photos she had taken with her new digital camera would help her remember this visit to the city forever.

She smiled with a touch of wistfulness as she thought back over the past two weeks—of pleasant times spent chatting over breakfast with the other guests at the *pensione* or enjoying leisurely multicourse meals at one or another of Venice's canal-front open-air restaurants. That was one of the unexpected difficulties of the sort of

travel schedule she was following. Just when she started to get to know a new place, it was time to move on. Then again, she supposed she ought to be used to that. She'd spent much of her childhood moving around thanks to her parents' peripatetic jobs as landscape designers, and while she didn't feel nearly as nervous about traveling to a new city or country as she once had about starting a new school, she did still have the same type of sadness whenever she had to leave each newly familiar place behind. Still, she was starting to think that feeling was just a part of being alive and involved in your surroundings.

As the *vaporetto* headed down the canal toward the train station, she dug into her shoulder bag for her digital camera, a bon voyage gift from her parents when she'd left for Europe some three months earlier. Nicole had already filled the memory card at least five times, downloading the photos onto her laptop and selecting the best ones to e-mail to her family, Patrice, and various other friends. One of the only things she truly regretted about her previous trip to Europe was that she hadn't brought a camera. She had to rely mostly on her memory—along with a few pictures taken by other people—to help her remember the semester she'd spent in Paris.

Luckily, her memories were strong—sometimes a little *too* strong. For instance, it was all too easy to remember what a bad attitude she'd had about that semester in the beginning. She hadn't wanted to go to France at all. She hadn't wanted to spend the first semester of her senior year anywhere but back home in Peabody Corner, Maryland, with her boyfriend, Nate, and her three best friends.

It's a good thing Mom and Dad were so stubborn about forcing me to expand my horizons, she thought now with a slight shudder as she fiddled with the settings on her camera. *Otherwise I'd probably be at Nate's college right this second working on my M.R.S. degree.*

Eighteen months ago, that would have been all she could have dreamed of for her life. Nate Carlton had seemed the very picture of the ideal boyfriend—handsome, funny, smart enough, and always the life of the party. Nicole had been terrified that being away from him for three and a half months would change things between them. And, in fact, that was exactly what had happened. At first it had seemed like a disaster when Nate had dumped her. But Nicole realized it was the best thing that could have happened to her. Now, almost exactly a year after the end of her Paris semester, she could hardly imagine what it had been like to be that girl—the girl who pictured nothing more exciting out of her life than marriage, a family, and a nice house in the suburbs.

She gazed out at the Venetian scenery, hardly seeing the palazzi, bridges, and gondolas they were passing as she pondered the person she'd been back then. She was a whole different person now, that was for sure. That

was why she'd decided to postpone college for a year to see a little more of the world. Fortunately, her parents had been thrilled by the idea and were helping her as much as they could with expenses. After a summer spent working three jobs to earn the additional funds she would need, Nicole had arrived in London back in mid-August. After spending some time in that bustling, vibrant city, she'd traveled to nearby Ireland and Scotland before heading over to the Continent. She'd spent the past six weeks in Italy and planned to move on after the holidays and travel around Switzerland, Austria, Germany, and on from there.

And now back to Paris...She shivered, and only partly because of the breeze blowing over the water as the boat chugged on along the murky canal. Suddenly she couldn't wait to get back.

Patrice's face suddenly appeared over the edge of her sleeping compartment, peering upside down into Nicole's bunk below. "Good thing we're not claustrophobic!" she said with a giggle.

Nicole finished shoving her bags to the foot of her bunk, then rolled out and stood up, being careful not to bump her head on the bottom of Patrice's bunk. The two of them had the bottom two beds of the stack of three in the tiny, six-by-eight-foot sleeping compartment on the train. The berths folded away into seats for daytime use, but the girls had decided not to bother with changing the setup. They planned to get to sleep in a couple of hours to prepare for their arrival in Paris the next morning.

"I know what you mean," Nicole said, stretching as best she could in the narrow space. She glanced at the top bed, which was empty. "It's almost time to go. Looks like we might have this compartment to ourselves tonight."

"Cool." Patrice sat up. She was petite enough to do so without risking a bump on the head from the berth above. "Honestly, I was a little weirded out when I found out we might be sleeping with some stranger."

"That's how I felt the first time, too," Nicole admitted as her friend hopped down to join her. "But most of the people who travel this way are really friendly. You get used to it."

She smiled as she remembered the jolly group of young Norwegians with whom she'd shared a six-person *couchette* compartment on the way from London to Rome, her first overnight train trip. They had spent the early part of the evening practicing their English on her by trying to tell dirty jokes, with Nicole laughingly doing her best to correct them using a combination of English and what little Swedish she'd picked up from her S.A.S.S. friend Annike, which the Norwegians mostly seemed to understand. The guys in the group had spent the night snoring loudly in harmony.

Patrice shot her an admiring glance. "You know, sometimes you amaze me, Nic," she joked. "I mean, are you

really the same girl who wouldn't change your clothes in gym class if anyone was looking?"

"I guess not." Nicole returned her smile. She slung her handbag over her shoulder. "Come on, let's go outside and look out the window—we should be leaving soon."

They left the sleeping compartment. Outside, dozens of other travelers were standing at the windows that lined the narrow aisleway running down the right-hand side of the sleeping car. The passengers were chatting and laughing in a variety of languages and accents. A trio of middle-aged Italians had the windows open and were chattering rapidly with a big group of people out on the platform. Nearby, half a dozen scruffy student types had their arms around one another's shoulders and were singing "Fratelli d'Italia," the national anthem of Italy, in a mixture of Italian, French, and English.

Patrice's dark eyes were round as she looked around. "Wow," she said. "This is really something."

Nicole knew exactly how she felt, because she remembered feeling the same way herself. Taking the trains in Europe, especially the less expensive cars, reminded her of the way she'd felt when walking into her S.A.S.S. classrooms for the first time. It reminded her that here, she was the foreigner, the one who didn't speak the language and had to rely on the kindness of strangers, along with her own resourcefulness, just to get by. Being here made her wish she'd paid more attention to the foreign exchange students she'd encountered during her high school years. But back then, she'd been too wrapped up in her own life even to notice them most of the time.

Just then a whistle blew, and a cheer went up from the passengers. "Blimey! We're off!" a girl at the far end of the car cried out in a strong British accent, eliciting laughter from all around. Several excited-looking blond teenagers started loudly singing what Nicole could only guess was a Christmas carol in what she thought might be Polish.

For a moment she felt a pang, realizing that Christmas was almost here. She'd mostly been too busy in her travels to be homesick, but with the holidays approaching, she was starting to feel it a little. By now, the reindeer and Christmas tree would be up on the roof of the Peabody Diner back home and that house on Calvert Street would be soaking up half the electricity on the eastern seaboard trying to get their elaborate holiday light display featured on the local news again…

She sighed. It didn't matter. It wasn't as if her parents would be there this Christmas, either. They had accepted a new garden-design commission in New Mexico. It was a short-term job this time, which meant they hadn't had to actually move there and could keep their home in Peabody Corner. But it also meant they would be working straight through the holidays and halfway into January. Nicole had looked into flying there to spend Christmas week with them but had quickly given up on the idea. Flights

were hard to come by that time of year and prohibitively expensive, and Nicole was on a tight budget—flying back to the U.S. for that one week would have meant cutting her travels short by at least a month.

In any case, her parents had pointed out that they would be too busy to spend much time with Nicole before their job was finished. Instead, they planned to fly over when Nicole got to Germany the following month and celebrate together then. Okay, so maybe it was a little lame to have Christmas in late January, but oh well.

Besides, it all worked out just fine, Nicole thought with a shiver of anticipation. *If I have to be away from my real home for the holidays, at least I get to spend that time in my home-away-from-home—Paris.*

Patrice giggled and applauded as the Polish teens finished their carol and started another. "This is fun! Definitely way more festive than Amtrak, huh?"

Nicole pulled her camera out of her bag. A cute, dark-haired guy around her age saw her and gestured for her to take his place at the window so she could get some better shots.

"Thanks," she said, stepping forward. *"Grazie. Merci."*

The guy responded in some language she didn't recognize. But judging by his smile and admiring look, she was pretty sure he'd understood her just fine.

"Ooh," Patrice whispered, crowding up to join her at the

window. "Leave it to you to pick up a cute guy within seconds of getting on the train!"

Nicole stuck out her tongue at her friend. She was aware that her blond, all-American good looks tended to attract male attention everywhere she went. But she tried not to think about that too much, except to be grateful when it occasionally helped her out of a jam. It was what it was.

She snapped a few photos of Venice as the train slowly picked up speed. Then the smiling dark-haired guy stepped forward and tapped her on the shoulder. "I take photo you girls?" he said in heavily accented pidgin English, adding a few helpful gestures to make himself more clear.

"Sure, thanks." Nicole handed him the camera, then put her arm around Patrice and posed for the picture.

"Say mozzarella!" Patrice said as the camera clicked.

Nicole laughed. "We're leaving Italy now," she reminded her. "You'll have to start saying 'say Camembert' or something instead."

"I'm not sure I can," Patrice joked. "At least not with that kind of accent."

"Well, you can just practice saying this instead." Nicole glanced out the window at the sight of watery, wonderful Venice sliding away outside. *"Arrivaderci* Venice, *Bonjour* Paris!"

Chapter Two

"*Bonjour*, anybody home?" Nicole pushed open the door to the S.A.S.S.-provided flat to which she'd been assigned. Inside she got a brief impression of a small room with pale green walls and dark furniture. But that view was quickly blocked by a blur of flying blond hair and smiling face flinging itself at her. Nicole dropped her bags just in time. "Annike!" she exclaimed with a grin. "You're already here!"

Annike had been the very first S.A.S.S. classmate Nicole had met in Paris. At first she had been awed by the Swedish girl's effortless sophistication, her language skills, and her fashion-model good looks, but Annike's natural charm and enthusiasm had quickly won her over. By the end of the semester, the two of them were great friends. Annike had even come to the United States to visit Nicole over the summer. It had been fun to show her around Peabody Corner, as well as nearby Washington, D.C., and Nicole planned to wind up her year of travels in Stockholm so Annike could return the favor. In the meantime, that surprise letter from S.A.S.S. had given them the unexpected opportunity to see each other in between.

"Nicole!" Annike cried, squeezing her into a hug so tight it took Nicole's breath away. "*Ça va?* You are here at last!"

"Ça va bien!" Nicole returned the hug, then stood back and held her by both shoulders. "It's so good to see you again!"

Annike looked as beautiful as ever. Her shoulder-length light blond hair and sparkling blue eyes were set off by a stylish blue sweater and a pair of delicate silver hoop earrings, and her long, slim legs were encased in faded jeans.

As Patrice stepped into the apartment behind Nicole, Annike turned to her with a welcoming smile. "*Bienvenue à Paris,* Patrice," she said. "It is wonderful to see you again, too. I still feel that I did not thank you enough for helping Nicole to show me around last summer—I had such a marvelous time on my first visit to the States!"

"No problem, it was fun." Patrice walked a little farther into the room and glanced around. "Thanks for letting me crash here tonight. Especially since it looks like there's barely room for the two of you." She giggled.

"I only wish you could stay longer," Annike said in her lightly accented English. "I believe you have never before been to Paris?"

"I haven't," Patrice said. "Actually, I've never been anywhere before now, except Ottawa—that's in Canada. My aunt and uncle live up there." She shrugged. "I just wish I had more time to spend here—from everything Nicole has ever told me, it sounds so wonderful and romantic!"

Nicole shot her friend a fond smile. That was just like Patrice to remember only the positive things she'd heard about Paris. *It's not as if I didn't do plenty of complaining about the place at first,* she thought.

"Well, at least you get a couple of days, and that is better than nothing," Annike said. "Although this city is so fantastic, there is far too much to see for only one day—or even one month!"

Patrice's eyes widened. "Tell me about it!" she exclaimed. "I saw so many cool things on the way here from the train station that I thought I was going to die. I mean, come on—how crazy is it to come around a corner and look up and see the freaking Eiffel Tower?"

"Oh, but you can see all of the Tower that you like." Annike gestured toward the pair of narrow windows in the wall opposite the door. "We have quite a nice view of it from here."

"Really?" Patrice dropped her bags and rushed to the windows. "Oh my gosh, you're right! That's so amazing!"

Nicole dragged her bags over out of the way, then shrugged off her coat and flopped down on the squishy brown sofa that took up almost half of the tiny main room. "It's so weird to be back in Paris, isn't it?" she said as Annike sat down beside her. "Especially at this time of year. It sort of feels like I never left."

"I understand exactly what you mean." Annike smiled. "In some sense, everything is so much the same—the buildings and landmarks, the holiday window displays, the people rushing about. Yet in other ways it is all so very different. Then again, perhaps it is we who are most different, *ja*?"

"Yeah, maybe you're right," Nicole agreed. "Still, not everything here is the same. Just on the way here I noticed that one coffee shop we used to go to over near the train station has been replaced by some kind of doggy boutique!" She smiled fondly at the memory of how much Parisians loved their pet pooches. "Weird to think of a place like Paris ever changing, but I guess it does."

"Excuse me, guys." Patrice turned away from the window. "Or maybe I should say excuse-ay-moi? Uh, how do you say 'where's the bathroom' in French?" She crossed one leg over the other and giggled. "I've been holding it

for hours—once our train got within sight of Paris, I sort of forgot about everything else!"

Annike laughed. "One would ask, *Où est la salle de bain?* And the answer is, *C'est tout droit.*" She pointed to a door across the room. "Straight through there and then to the left. Be warned, though—it is quite small!"

"Hey, as long as the toilet is regulation size, I don't care!" Patrice giggled again, then scooted out through the door.

Annike turned back to Nicole. "And you?" she said. "What has changed for you since we have spoken, Nicole? How are your travels getting on?"

"Great! I loved Italy, even though my attempts to pick up some of the language were pretty pathetic." Nicole laughed. "I took Spanish in high school, remember? So I was always trying to speak that since it's so similar, then remembering at the last minute and getting all tongue-tied..."

Annike chuckled. "I have the same trouble remembering not to speak my little bit of Norwegian when I visit Denmark."

Nicole smiled admiringly. Even after a full semester in Paris and three additional months of traveling, it seemed impossible that she would ever be as cosmopolitan as her sweet, sophisticated Swedish friend.

"What about you?" she asked Annike. "How are things with Berg?"

Annike blushed and ducked her head to hide a smile, which gave Nicole all the answer she needed. Berg was

Annike's boyfriend of two months. She'd met him at her university back in Sweden, where she had started her undergraduate degree that autumn.

"Things are very good," Annike said. "Berg, he is a good, smart person, and very sweet to me. We are getting on quite well." She shot Nicole a glance. "You might get to meet him. He is going to try to come down and join us here in Paris for a few days after Christmas."

Nicole sat up straight. "Awesome!" she exclaimed. "I can't wait to meet him. From everything you've told me, he sounds like such a great guy. I'm so glad you're happy with him."

"Oh yes, things are still very good with Berg and me," Annike said. "Yes, there is nothing new to report *there.*"

"Cool." Nicole peered at her, noticing the odd emphasis Annike had put on the last word and the funny little half smile on her lips. "Wait, what do you mean nothing to report *there*? Is there something to report somewhere else? Come on—spill!"

Patrice emerged back into the room at that moment. She stared at Nicole and Annike curiously. "Spill what?" she asked, hurrying over and perching on the arm of the sofa. "Am I missing some juicy gossip?"

"Well... perhaps." Annike cleared her throat, her expression wavering between enthusiasm and uncertainty. "I was about to tell Nicole my interesting news. I seem to have been, how would one say it? Er, discovered?"

"What?" Nicole blinked, then leaned forward to peer into Annike's face. "Wait, do you mean *discovered* discovered? As in welcome to Hollywood, and the Oscar goes to Annike?" She was already imagining it in full Technicolor. With Annike's cool, classic Swedish good looks and winning personality, it was really a miracle it hadn't happened already. "I can't believe it—I'll totally be able to say I knew you when!"

Annike held up both hands and laughed. "*Vänta!* It's nothing quite so glamorous as that!" she said. "Let me explain. I was walking in Stockholm several weeks ago when a man stopped me. It happened that he was from the BBC. He was a—er, what would be the English word? One in search of people to put on his shows?"

"A talent scout!" Patrice was wide-eyed again, hanging on Annike's every word.

"Yes, a scout—that is exactly how he referred to himself." Annike nodded, seeming pleased with the vocabulary reminder. "He was in search of contestants for a brand-new reality television program called *International Relations*."

"A reality show? Cool!" Nicole said. "What's it going to be about? Are you going to do it? When do you start? Wow, this is so incredible! I can't believe I'm going to know a TV star!"

"Ach, give me a chance to answer!" Annike cried with a laugh. "Firstly, the show will involve a bunch of young people from all over the world. They will stay in a house together in London for six months or so, living according to different cultures. For instance, one week everyone might have to eat only the traditional foods of India. On another day, they might be required to wear traditional Moroccan *djellabas* or learn an Argentine tango or other things. The contestants will also be taking part in academic challenges to test their knowledge of other places, and such as that." She shrugged. "This scout, he talked to me awhile and thought I might be a good candidate to represent Scandinavia. He wants me to come to London next month to do a screen test."

"Oh, wow!" Nicole exclaimed. "That show sounds *perfect* for you! I mean, you're so interested in traveling, and your language skills are—What?" she interrupted herself, noticing the conflicted expression on her friend's face. "Why don't you seem more excited about this?"

"Maybe she's already jaded." Patrice giggled. "It's probably totally boring talking about it with us little people."

That made Annike laugh a little. "No, trust me, Patrice, it is not that at all." She shrugged and glanced over at Nicole. "It is true, if I were to be chosen for the program, it would be a very exciting experience. It combines many of the things I love most—traveling, meeting new people, learning new things."

"So what's the problem?" Nicole was a bit puzzled by Annike's relatively subdued response. If *she'd* been

chosen for such a cool-sounding TV show, she'd be shouting it from the rooftops!

"As I said, the show will go on for at least six months, beginning next August," Annike said. "It would mean dropping out of school—at least for a while—and moving to London for the duration."

Patrice looked sympathetic. "I get it," she said, patting Annike on the arm. "Is it your boyfriend? Nicole showed me pictures—trust me, *I* wouldn't want to leave that behind for long, either."

"Berg is being very supportive," Annike said, shaking her head. "He just says it is my decision to make. He thinks I need to do what is best for me."

"What do your parents say?" Nicole asked.

"I have not told them of this yet," Annike admitted. "However, I know already what they will say. They will want me to finish my education first. And perhaps they are right." She brushed back a strand of blond hair that had fallen forward over her face. "But how can I pass this by? Such an opportunity might never come to me again. And it would be such fun."

"Yeah." Nicole wasn't sure what to say. Part of her wanted to urge Annike to accept the offer. After all, she was right—how often did anyone have the chance to do something like that? Then again, she didn't want to push her friend into anything she wasn't sure about. Nicole had spent enough time back in high school being pushed into things by her friends. Her semester abroad hadn't only helped her to see that Nate was all wrong for her. It had also made her see the same thing about her other two best friends, Zara and Annie. After all the moving around she'd had to do in her younger years, Nicole had been so grateful to have the two popular girls fold her into their group that she hadn't stopped to realize that maybe they didn't really act like true friends a lot of the time—especially Zara.

All that had changed after Nicole's time in Paris. The first time Zara had made some snide little comment about France after Nicole's return, Nicole had shut her down. Zara had been so shocked that she hadn't really responded at the time—most people didn't dare talk back to the mighty Zara Adams. But after that, the friendship was essentially over. It hadn't been easy to survive the cold stares and whispered gossip that had followed. But Nicole and Patrice had leaned on each other to get through it, and now, with high school almost six months behind them, it already seemed like little more than a distant memory.

Patrice looked confused. "But you could go back to school later, right?" she asked Annike. "So really, you could do both."

"I suppose." Annike looked slightly troubled. "But it is not quite so simple as that. As I said, the commitment to the program would be at least six months, with a possibility of more. I would have to withdraw from the university

and give up my flat—ach, there would be much to think of. In any case, I do not have long to decide. I am supposed to let them know by the end of next week—just after Christmas."

"It's okay." Nicole leaned over to give her a hug. "I'm here to talk it out if you want."

Annike smiled at her. "*Merci,* Nicole," she said. "You are a good friend. It is so nice to be here with you once more."

"Ditto." Nicole was about to ask more questions about the TV show when there came a faint buzzing sound from the direction of her shoulder bag, which she'd shrugged off upon entering the apartment.

"There's your phone," Patrice said, hurrying over to grab it out of Nicole's bag.

Nicole caught it as Patrice tossed it to her. Flipping it open, she answered on the fourth ring. "Hello?"

"*Allô? Je voudrais parler à* the most beautiful girl in the world, *s'il vous plaît*?"

"Luc! *Ça va?*" Nicole felt a funny little thrill run through her. It had been a long time since she'd heard Luc's voice, but it was still instantly familiar.

"Je vais bien," Luc responded. "I am at work at the restaurant, so I sadly cannot speak for long at this moment. But I wished to be certain to welcome you back to Paris."

"Thanks. It's good to be back." Nicole did her best to ignore Patrice, who was making goofy kissy faces in between muffled giggles. Annike looked amused as she glanced back and forth between Patrice and Nicole.

"*Tu es libre* this evening, *chérie*?" Luc asked. "If so, perhaps we shall be together for dinner? And of course, you should bring the lovely Mademoiselle Annike, and your friend from the States as well. We shall all have a wonderful time."

"That sounds great." Nicole lowered the phone. "Hey, guys, want to get together with Luc tonight for dinner?"

"Ça serait génial," Annike said with a nod.

Patrice smirked. "Do you even need to ask?"

Nicole rolled her eyes at her friend, then raised the phone again. "We're on," she told Luc. "When and where?"

After making the arrangements, Luc had to go back to work. Nicole hung up and turned to face her friends, who were both smiling at her.

"So," Nicole said, tossing the phone back on top of her bags. "What were we talking about? Oh yeah—Annike's show."

Annike waved her slim hands as if shooing away a fly. "Enough of that topic for the moment," she said. "I have been thinking of nothing else and it is making me *snurrig i huvudet*. Why discuss it when we could instead be discussing so many other things after so long apart?"

"Right!" Patrice joined in eagerly. "Like that dinner tonight. I can't believe I'm finally going to meet Monsieur Romance in person!"

Annike laughed. "*Ja,* it will be nice to see him again. But do not expect him to pay much attention to you," she warned Patrice jokingly. "Oh, he will be polite, of course. Perhaps even flirt a little. But when Nicole is around, he has eyes for no one else."

Nicole could feel her cheeks going pink. "Stop it, you guys," she muttered. "It's not like that with Luc and me. You know that."

She did her best to shake off her romantic flutters over Luc. It was silly to get so worked up over seeing him again. Yes, they'd had a few...special moments in the past. But that was just what it was—*in the past.* After all, she was no giddy schoolgirl waiting for some handsome Prince Charming to sweep her off her feet. Not anymore.

Luc is just a friend, she reminded herself. *He's the guy who helped me grow up and learn to stand on my own two feet. The guy who made me see that my future didn't have to be the way I'd always assumed it would be. That's more than enough.*

"We shall see," Annike said with a twinkle in her eye. "It is true, last year there were many complications for you two, and so you never quite became—how do you say it?—involved together? But now things are different. This time there is nothing stopping you from seeing what shall happen between the two of you."

For just a moment Nicole allowed herself to imagine it.

The last time she'd been in Paris, things had indeed been complicated. First she'd been with Nate, and then by the time they'd broken up, the semester was nearly over. Even so, she and Luc had had a few close encounters that still made her heart beat a little faster when she thought of them.

She smiled, remembering how he would gaze at her with those intense yet playful green eyes as he tossed off some incomprehensible French quip. She had met him on her first day in Paris—at the time he had been the Smiths' nanny, which had meant he'd always seemed to be around. He'd flirted with her unmercifully despite knowing she had a boyfriend back home. At first she'd found his *laissez-faire* attitude toward life and love maddening. But after a while she had come to appreciate his unique take on the world. It had been kind of nice to hang out with someone who always seemed to have all the time in the world to spend with her and all the interest in the world in whatever she had to say.

Still, she knew she shouldn't expect too much of this brief visit. Since the Smiths had moved to Hong Kong, Luc had told Nicole in past e-mails that he'd taken on several part-time jobs—as a waiter, a part-time babysitter, and a proofreader—to support himself and pay for his university courses. After tonight's dinner, she would probably be lucky if he had enough time off to meet her for coffee a

couple of times during her two weeks in Paris.

Nicole stood up, not quite meeting Annike's eye. "Some things are different," she said. "But one thing is definitely the same. Luc and I are friends—nothing more."

Patrice looked skeptical. "Okay. So that's why you turn into a beet every time someone mentions his name."

"A beet?" Annike glanced at Patrice curiously. "How do you mean?"

"It's a vegetable. She's just being silly," Nicole said. "And don't be ridiculous, you guys. I'm only here for like two weeks—hardly enough time for the romance of the century you two seem to be imagining." That thought brought her down to earth. What was the point of even dreaming about turning her friendship with Luc into anything more? It was totally impractical. She shrugged and shot a look at Annike. "Anyway, you know Luc. He probably has a whole collection of girlfriends."

Patrice looked ready to continue the teasing, but Annike stood up and stretched gracefully. "If you say so, my friend," she said. "But come—let us put your bags in the bedroom and then we can begin to show Patrice more of Paris."

Nicole was relieved by the change of topic. Still, even as she helped the other girls drag the suitcases out of the tiny sitting room into the equally tiny bedroom, she couldn't quite get the sound of Luc's playful, familiar voice out of her head.

Chapter Three

"Are we there yet?" Patrice asked with a mock groan.

Nicole laughed. "Almost."

"Sorry for walking your feet off today, Patrice," Annike put in sympathetically. "But you have only one and one-half days to see Paris, and we will all be busy at the video shoot tomorrow. So we did not want you to miss anything too important today."

Nicole pushed back her coat sleeve to check her watch. "Come on, we'd better keep moving," she said. "We were supposed to meet Luc ten minutes ago. You can rest your feet when we get to the restaurant."

Patrice groaned again. "Oh, all right. But just so you know, it's only the thought of meeting Monsieur Hottie McFrenchy that's keeping me going!"

The three girls were hurrying along the sidewalk in a bustling shopping and dining district in the eleventh *arrondissement.* The sun had set some time ago, but the street was aglow, not only with the street lamps and other ordinary lights of the city, but also the twinkling strands of holiday lights strung up outside some of the cafés and other businesses. The evening air was not quite as cold as a typical December night back in Maryland, but it was chilly and a bit damp.

Even wrapped in winter clothes, Annike managed to look sleek and stylish. She wore a tailored black wool coat that was about half the volume of Nicole's puffy down jacket, along with a cheerful bright green hat and scarf. She wrapped both arms around herself and sighed happily as she glanced around at the busy Paris street. "It is so wonderful to be back, isn't it?"

"Totally," Nicole replied. "Seeing the sights reminds me of my first few weeks here." She shot Patrice a sly glance. "It's just too bad we didn't have time to show you the Paris Sewer Museum."

Patrice looked confused. "Ew. What? Does the word *sewer* mean something else in French, I hope?"

Annike let out a shout of laughter. "Ah yes, remember the field trip we took there in Artist's Eye?"

Annike was referring to a class she and Nicole had taken together. Its full name was Paris Through an Artist's Eye. It was an art appreciation class, but beyond that, it was supposed to help students learn to see the world more creatively. It had ended up being Nicole's favorite class of the semester.

"Yeah. We went there the same day we visited the Père Lachaise cemetery," Nicole said. "Talk about a lot of walking! My feet were ready to fall off by the end of the trip."

"Ah, yes." Annike laughed. "Thinking of that day reminds me also of those Irish boys from the class—Seamus and Finn, remember them? They were quite silly at the Sewer Museum."

"How could I forget?" Nicole shook her head, thinking fondly of the pair. "They spoke of nothing but Parisian poo for weeks afterward."

"Yes. And then there was the time they—Oh, but listen to me go on!" Annike interrupted herself, shooting Patrice an apologetic look. "So sorry, Patrice. Here we are chattering on about people and places and leaving you out of the conversation entirely."

"It's okay," Patrice replied with a smile. "I know you guys have a lot of catching up to do. I don't mind—I'm just walking along all overwhelmed by Paris anyway. Oh, and trying to survive my aching feet, of course."

They had just turned a corner onto the street where they were supposed to meet Luc in front of a trendy

Parisian bistro. Glancing ahead, Nicole saw a familiar tall, lean figure standing on the curb gazing across the street, rocking back and forth against the cold with both hands shoved into the pockets of his jacket.

Annike spotted him a moment later. "Ah, there is Luc," she said. "He looks as handsome as ever, does he not, Nicole?"

Nicole didn't answer. She had just flashed back to the first time she'd laid eyes on Luc. That encounter had taken place during the daytime in a completely different *arrondissement*. But then as now, she had spotted him from halfway down the block. And then as now, she'd been completely distracted by Luc's spiky dark hair, his intense green eyes, that little smile that always seemed to be playing around his lips...

Before she could stop it, her mind drifted to the memory of their first kiss. It had taken place among the magnificent gardens at Versailles and had lasted only a moment, but Nicole still remembered the little shudder that had gone through her like an electric shock at the feel of his lips on hers.

At that moment Luc turned and spotted them. His face lit up as he hurried to meet them. *"Bonsoir!"* he called. "There you are!"

Nicole shook off her memories. It was no wonder she had slid into them on seeing Luc, just as she'd been nearly overwhelmed by memories at seeing Paris again. That was perfectly normal. She'd flashed back to some good memories with Nate the first time she'd seen him after they'd broken up, too, but that hadn't meant she wanted to revive things between them.

"Hi," she said as Luc bent to kiss her on both cheeks in the French manner, then wrapped his long arms around her for a hug. "It's good to see you. Sorry we're late."

"Mieux vaut tard que jamais," he murmured in her ear, his breath hot against her cold cheek. "I would have waited all night for you, *chérie*." But he almost immediately loosened his grip, turning to greet Annike with seemingly equal enthusiasm.

Nicole reached for Patrice's hand. When Luc and Annike had finished saying hello, she pulled her friend forward.

"This is Patrice," she said. "Patrice, this is Luc."

"Ah, *mais bien sûr*." Luc took Patrice's hand and kissed it, then bent down to kiss her on both cheeks as well. "Nicole has told me a great deal about you. However, she failed to express exactly how beautiful you are."

"Ditto." Patrice giggled. "And, uh, *merci*. Is that how you say it? Totally nice to meet you, Luc."

Nicole could tell that her friend was a bit disarmed by Luc, and no wonder. There weren't many guys like him back home in Peabody Corner!

"Come on, let's go inside," she said with a shiver. "It's cold out here."

Soon the four of them were settled at a table along the back wall of the charming candlelit restaurant. Soft music mingled with the sounds of voices, laughter, and clinking tablewear, and the air was scented with garlic and various other enticing aromas.

"So tell me of this video that has brought you here," Luc said, leaning back in his chair and smiling at the girls. "Shall you be putting on costumes and performing skits?"

Annike laughed. "Nothing like that, I hope," she said. "They just want to film us for the S.A.S.S. Web site. Part of the time we will be reading a script about some new programs, but mostly I think we are supposed to give our true impressions of our experiences with the S.A.S.S. program and what we have learned from being here and such as that."

"Ah, I see." Luc shot Nicole a glance. "It is no wonder they wanted the two of you to take part. Who could resist joining a program where one might meet such beautiful girls?"

Patrice giggled. "Okay, I know I only just met you, Luc. But I can't help noticing that you seem to think *all* girls are beautiful."

Luc smiled at her, his green eyes glittering with amusement in the light of the candles on their table. "Ah, but it is true," he said. "Not all girls are blessed with the God-given beauty of the three of you, *naturellement*. But there is some beauty in everyone. *Tous les goûts sont dans la nature*."

Just then the waiter arrived at the table. He was a tall, lanky, good-looking young man in his twenties with a shock of blond hair and startlingly pink, cherublike cheeks in an otherwise pale and chiseled face.

"Vous avez choisi?" he asked. Then he noticed Luc. "Ah! Luc, *mon ami*..." He then launched into an enthusiastic torrent of French so rapid that Nicole couldn't quite follow it, though she gathered the two of them had been in school together at some point. She traded an amused glance with Annike. Sometimes it seemed that Luc knew everyone in Paris!

"Shall I order for us, ladies?" Luc asked, glancing around the table. "I know this place well, and between my friend Gilles and myself, we should be able to put together an interesting meal to please everyone."

"Sounds like a plan," Nicole said as Annike nodded agreeably.

Patrice shrugged. "Go for it. I wouldn't have any idea what to order, anyway."

Luc consulted with the waiter. Once again, their French was so rapid that Nicole could hardly follow it.

"Wow," she murmured to Annike. "My French is getting rusty. Too much time away, I guess."

Annike smiled sympathetically. "It will come back soon enough, I am sure. I already feel mine improving after just one day."

At the end of his discussion with Gilles, Luc paused and

glanced around. "May I treat us to a nice bottle of wine?" he asked. "After all, it is a special occasion."

"Can we do that?" Patrice giggled. "Um, I mean, back home we're still too young to drink. You know—legally."

Luc winked at her. "But you are in France now, *chérie*," he said. "We are not so uptight about such things here."

Patrice blushed. "Well, then, if you insist..."

"Indeed I do." Luc shot her a wicked grin, then turned back to the waiter and ordered the wine.

Nicole smiled at Patrice. "Having fun?"

"Oui oui!" Patrice replied happily. "This day has been amazing. I mean, this place—it's so—so—*Paris*. I can't believe I'm really here, you know?"

Luc and Annike chuckled. "I felt the same way when I first visited," Annike said. "I think everyone does."

"Right," Nicole agreed. "Although I have to admit, Patrice, you have a much better attitude than I did when I first came here." She shook her head, remembering how resistant she had been to the whole idea of Paris. "Then again, you came by choice!"

"Ah, how I remember," Luc said. "At first, our Nicole wanted nothing to do with Paris. But we won her over in the end, eh?"

Nicole smiled. She was definitely feeling a buzz from seeing Luc again. But she figured that was only natural. Who could resist a little romantic nostalgia at a time like this? Maybe even a little harmless flirting? It didn't have to mean anything.

Luc leaned forward and gazed across the table at Patrice. "You have chosen a wonderful time of year to visit Paris," he told her. "The city, it is special at any season. But at the holidays, it holds an even more incredible charm."

"Yeah, we saw a lot of the decorations while we were walking around today. They're beautiful." Patrice grinned and glanced at Nicole. "Much classier than the giant moth-eaten Rudolph on top of the diner back home, huh, Nic?"

Nicole chuckled, though Luc and Annike looked slightly perplexed. At that moment the waiter reappeared bearing their wine and a tray of appetizers. Luc clapped his hands with approval.

"Ah, wonderful," he said. "*J'ai une faim de loup.* I hope everyone will enjoy what I have ordered."

Patrice watched as Gilles poured her a glass of red wine. "Thanks," she said. "Er, I mean, *merci.*" She giggled and glanced at Luc. "Sorry, I don't know much French."

"C'est pas grand-chose," Luc responded. "Charm and beauty translate to any language."

Nicole could tell that Patrice wasn't quite sure what to say to that, and not just because of the French. She knew how she felt—Luc could be a bit overwhelming. True to form, though, Patrice didn't stay tongue-tied for long.

"Cheers, everyone," she said, lifting her glass and taking a sip.

"Skål," Annike said, raising her own glass.

"Santé," Luc added. "That is how we say it here in France."

Patrice laughed and took another drink. "It's amazing," she said. "Back home, you don't really think about how many different languages there are in the world. But here we all are!" She glanced around the restaurant. "It's kind of crazy to realize that people everywhere are really kind of the same—yet so different in some ways, too."

"Sort of like the holidays, I guess," Nicole said. "Hey, Patrice, did you know that here in France little kids don't hang stockings for Santa? Instead they put their shoes out so that Père Noël can fill them with candy and treats." At Luc's surprised look, she smiled smugly. "See, I did learn a few things from being here last year."

"*Oui, un soulier de Noël.* Very good. But did you stay long enough last year to taste a *bûche de Noël*?" Luc licked his lips. "It is not truly Christmas until one has tasted it. And of course one must look forward to *le réveillon*—that is the feast we enjoy on Christmas Eve—*la veille de Noël*."

"Sounds like an awful lot of French Christmas traditions revolve around food. Just like at home!" Patrice took another sip of wine and reached for one of the appetizer plates. "So what's Christmas like in Sweden, Annike? Do you guys have Santa Claus there?"

Annike nodded. "Yes, but we also have Tomte the Christmas gnome," she said. "For us, Christmas really begins on the thirteenth of December. That's Saint Lucia's day. Then two days before Christmas, we set up our trees and decorate them with apples and candles."

"And goats, *non*?" Luc put in with a smile.

"Yes, and goats." Annike laughed. Seeing that both Nicole and Patrice wore confused expressions, she explained, "Luc is referring to the Julbok, or yule goat. They are very popular at home; you often see them made of straw and red ribbons."

"Oh right, I think I've seen those," Patrice said, reaching for her wineglass. "They sell them at this little Scandinavian shop at the beach back home."

She and Annike continued chatting about Swedish and American traditions. Meanwhile Luc leaned toward Nicole.

"The Smiths, they wanted me to be certain to wish you a happy Christmas on their behalf, Nicole," he said. "They sent you a holiday card from Hong Kong, but realize you probably shall not see it until you return home. But they wish you to know they are thinking of you."

Nicole smiled at the thought of her host family. "I'm thinking of them, too," she said. "I wish they were still here in Paris. I'd love to see them."

Luc took a sip of his wine and nodded. "I miss them, too. They were always very kind to me—working for them was one of my favorite jobs."

"You were good at it, too." Nicole chuckled at the memories of watching Luc wrangle all four of the Smith children at once, seemingly without breaking a sweat. "Those kids adored you. Bet they're giving their new nanny in Hong Kong a hard time!"

Luc laughed. "I do not doubt it. In any case, my three current jobs cannot compare."

"Right," Nicole said. "For instance, I assume most of them don't involve anyone wiping their runny nose on you?"

"*Oui,* this is mostly true!" He laughed again. "Then again, none of them have surprised me with a most generous bit of cash inside a holiday card as the Smiths did this year." He cleared his throat and shrugged, suddenly looking a bit sheepish, as if he'd said more than he'd intended. "Mr. and Mrs. Smith, they were always most interested in my schooling, you see, and they know that my mother does not have enough money to help me as much as she would like..."

Nicole nodded, taking a sip of her wine to avoid having to answer right away. It was obvious that Luc hadn't intended to mention the cash gift from the Smiths, and she could tell he wasn't terribly comfortable now that he'd let it slip. She knew that his widowed mother didn't have a lot of money—that was why he had to take on three jobs to help pay his way through school—but he never complained about it, and in fact seemed to prefer not to discuss it at all.

"Speaking of your mother, how is she doing these days?" she asked. "Is she still working at that dress shop?"

He seemed grateful for the change of subject. "Ah, yes, she is ever the same," he responded with a wave of his hand. "But what of your family? Tell me about this garden they are creating. It is in New Mexico, did you say in your e-mail? Do they have something against the old Mexico?"

Patrice turned toward him just in time to hear the joking question. She giggled. "Oh, I don't know," she joked in return. "Do you wonder the same thing about New Jersey and New York?"

"Absolument," Luc confirmed with a straight face. "Ever since you Americans have left the Old World, you insist upon everything new!"

That made them all laugh, and set off a round of good-natured teasing from both sides. A few minutes after that, the main courses arrived. As the others exclaimed over the food and then continued their conversation, Nicole felt a bit distracted. Luc's mention of the Smiths' Christmas gift had reminded her that she hadn't really done any Christmas shopping yet—she'd been so busy traveling that she hadn't had much time to think about it. On the few occasions that it *had* crossed her mind, she hadn't been too concerned, figuring she wouldn't need gifts for her parents until she saw them later in January. But what about her friends?

She shot a glance at Patrice, who looked pretty, pink-cheeked, and animated as she laughed at something Luc had just said. Nicole definitely wanted to get her something special this year. They'd been through a lot together and Nicole wanted her to know how much she appreciated her friendship.

And what about Annike? Nicole shifted her gaze to her Swedish friend. Annike was pretty special to her, too. It would be nice to get her something equally special.

Then there was Luc. Nicole hadn't really been planning to get him a gift, but being here with him now, she had started thinking that maybe she should.

She bit her lip and stared down at her plate. She really did want to let her friends know how much they meant to her. But she would have to be creative—her budget was pretty tight.

Oh well, she thought, reaching for another piece of bread. *I've got two whole weeks to work on it. If I can't find the perfect gifts in Paris, I'll have to turn in my expert shopper's badge!*

An hour later most of the food was gone. So was the entire bottle of wine—much of it into Patrice. Nicole had been so busy catching up with Luc and Annike that it had taken her a while to notice that her American friend had allowed Luc to refill her wineglass several times. By now, Patrice was obviously a bit tipsy.

"So, Luc," Patrice said, leaning forward on one elbow and grinning at him. "Did anyone ever tell you how adorable you are?"

Nicole winced, exchanging a quick look with Annike. Patrice didn't drink much back home, even now that she was in college. Obviously the wine had gone straight to her head.

But Luc smiled gallantly. "Ah, *tu me gâtes.* But it is an honor to hear such a thing from a beautiful lady such as yourself."

Patrice giggled, then let out a soft burp. That made her giggle even more. "Excuse-ay-moi," she said. "Hey Luc, is there a place to dance around here? We should totally go dance! I bet you have some moves, huh?" She wriggled her shoulders suggestively.

"Um, we'd better not," Nicole put in quickly. "Annike and I have to be at the shoot early tomorrow, remember?"

"Oops!" Patrice's eyes widened. She glanced from Nicole to Luc and back again. Then, leaning over toward Nicole, she added in a loud whisper, "Sorry, Nic! I totally didn't mean to make a play for your guy."

Nicole was glad the lighting in the restaurant was dim enough so that Luc probably couldn't see her blush. "You know, it's getting kind of late," she said. "Maybe we should wrap this up."

"Yes." Annike looked amused. "I am rather tired from our long day, aren't you, Patrice?"

"What? But we're just getting started!" Patrice giggled loudly. "Anyway, I want to talk to that cute waiter of ours about dessert. Hey, cute waiter! Yoo-hoo!" She waved her hand at Gilles, who was at another table nearby. Then she turned to Luc. "How do you say 'cute waiter' in French?"

"Come on." Nicole stood up, hooking her elbow through Patrice's and pulling her up as well. "I think I spotted a cute waiter back at the flat. Let's go check it out, okay?"

She couldn't help being a little embarrassed by Patrice's behavior. Still, she supposed that her friend was just having fun on her last night in Europe. What was the harm in that?

Luc stood, too. "Oh, must you really go already?"

"Yes, I think we'd better," Nicole said.

A few minutes later they were all outside on the sidewalk. It was colder now, and Nicole felt the damp air cut through her and make her shiver. But she felt a little warmer when Luc squeezed her tightly in a good-night hug.

"It is good to have you back, Nicole, even for such a short while," he said, his breath smelling of red wine and peppermint as he kissed her on the cheek. "I hope I shall see you again very soon."

Chapter Four

"Do you think Patrice will be all right to fly later today?" Annike asked as she and Nicole stepped onto the *métro* the next morning.

"I'm sure she'll be okay." Nicole yawned, glancing around the train car, which was crowded with morning commuters. "She just needs to sleep off some of that wine and then spend some time getting her things organized. I did most of her packing for her last night, since she was in no condition to do it. So at least that part shouldn't take her long."

She felt a rush of wistfulness as she thought about

Patrice leaving so soon. Any embarrassment she'd felt the evening before had passed quickly, and now all she could do was wish like crazy that her friend could stay a little longer. It wasn't fair—it seemed as if she'd just arrived, and now she had to go.

"Too bad she will not get to watch us filming today after all. She seemed rather excited by the idea." Annike clung to a pole as the *métro* rumbled into motion.

Nicole grabbed the same pole, her body automatically swaying with the movement of the train as it picked up speed. "I wonder what it's going to be like," she said. "I was so excited at the idea of coming back to Paris that I guess the actual filming was just sort of a footnote in my mind. I never really gave the details much thought."

"I have thought about it quite a lot, actually," Annike admitted. "This may sound rather stupid, but I have been thinking that this video shoot will be a sort of test for me—for that TV program, I mean." She smiled sheepishly. "I am hoping it will give me the feeling for what I could be in for if I say yes to the show. I realize it is not exactly the same thing," she added hastily, glancing over at Nicole. "But I wish to find out how I shall feel being the center of attention—having all eyes on me. I am not accustomed to that sort of thing, and I do not know whether I shall like it at all. That is why I fought so hard to come here for the holidays rather than staying at home as my family wished me to do."

Nicole couldn't help being a bit amazed. Annike was so gorgeous that it was hard to believe she could ever be bashful about having all eyes on her. Still, she supposed that being filmed was a different matter.

A few minutes later they stepped out of the Charles de Gaulle–Étoile *métro* station to find themselves on the Champs-Élysées, the world-famous Parisian avenue. Both sides of the street were strung with ropes of holiday lights, which twinkled weakly against the heavy, gray, overcast sky. A phone call the afternoon before had informed them that their first day's shooting would take place in front of the Arc de Triomphe, which stood nearby.

There weren't many tourists out so early, and they spotted the rest of their group as soon as they reached the open area around the massive stone Arc. Half a dozen other young people were milling around drinking coffee while, nearby, several burly men moved camera equipment.

"See anybody we know?" Nicole murmured as she and Annike approached. She scanned the group for familiar faces but didn't see any.

"I don't think anyone else from our program came back," Annike said. "I e-mailed the coordinator about it before I arrived, and you and I were the only ones."

The two of them soon located the director, a small, energetic British man named Nigel, and introduced themselves. He sent them over to wait with the others while the camera operators finished setting up.

"Hi there!" A stocky, broad-faced girl with bright red hair and a strong British accent hurried over as soon as Nicole and Annike approached the group. "I'm Quinn. Who are you?"

Nicole smiled uncertainly, a bit taken aback by the girl's rather blunt question. Meanwhile Annike spoke up to introduce the two of them and explain their backgrounds.

"First-semester Paris program last year, eh?" Quinn said. "Funny, that. I was *second*-semester Paris program last year. So was she." She jerked a thumb at a slender girl with mouse-brown hair who was standing nearby with both hands wrapped around a take-out coffee cup. "She's Yelena. She's from Russia, in case you couldn't tell from the name." Quinn laughed uproariously at her own comment.

Hearing her name, Yelena stepped forward and smiled uncertainly at Annike and Nicole. "Hello," she said in thickly accented English. "I am Yelena. You will be film with us, too?"

"That's right," Annike said. Then she added a sentence or two in what Nicole could only assume was Russian. She was surprised—she hadn't realized that was among the handful of languages her friend spoke.

Quinn looked surprised, too. "Oi," she said. "Listen, Yelena here's trying to improve her English, so let's stick with that, all right?"

"It is not a big deal," Annike said with a smile. "My Russian, it is not very good at all."

"No, no!" Yelena grinned eagerly at her. "You speak wonderful! It is very good."

Nicole smiled. She still remembered what a relief it had been whenever she'd heard someone speak English during her time in Paris, especially at the beginning of the semester when she hadn't yet started learning French.

"I wish I spoke any Russian at all," she told Yelena. "But the only phrase I know is, um, *das vendanya*? Is that how you say it?"

"It is said *das vee-da-nee-ye*," Yelena corrected with a smile. "But you were very close. It is meaning *au revoir*, good-bye."

"Listen," Quinn put in. "Are we going to stand here talking Russian all day, or do you want me to introduce the rest of this lot?" She waved a hand toward the other young people in their group, who were paying no attention to them whatsoever as they chatted among themselves a few yards away.

With some effort, Nicole managed to avoid rolling her eyes. She could already tell that Quinn was the type of person who wasn't happy unless she was the center of attention. "Sure," she said. "Let's go meet them."

The remaining members of their filming group for that day all turned out to be native Parisians who had studied with S.A.S.S. in other countries. One, a guy named Louis, had just returned from his semester in Munich. The other guy, Claude, had studied two years earlier in Mexico. The two girls, Sylvie and Adeline, had spent part of the previous year in Tokyo and Helsinki respectively. They were all nice enough, but after the introductions were complete, they seemed more interested in chatting with one another in French than in getting to know the others any better.

That left Nicole and Annike with Quinn and Yelena. Through further conversation—mostly dominated by Quinn—they learned that the pair hadn't really known each other during their shared semester in Paris. However, they'd recognized each other vaguely by sight when they'd arrived the day before and discovered that they would be rooming together for the duration of the filming.

Annike rubbed her hands together and glanced at the steaming cups in the other girls' hands. "Brr," she said. "Your coffees look good. May I ask, where did you get them?"

"Just across there." Quinn pointed to a shop across the avenue. "There's a very good café that's not too pricey."

"Shall we?" Annike glanced at Nicole, who nodded eagerly. "Right. If anyone asks, we'll be back in a moment."

Soon the two of them were hurrying through the underpass leading to the other side of the broad street. "That Quinn is something, huh?" Nicole commented. "I always think of British people as kind of polite, reserved, and dignified. Guess they're not *all* like that, huh?"

"Agreed." Annike chuckled as they emerged into the

open air and headed toward the café Quinn had indicated. "Yelena seems quite nice, though much quieter than her friend."

"I'm not sure I'd call them *friends*, exactly. I got the impression—Hold on a sec," Nicole interrupted herself as she heard the muffled sound of her cell phone from inside her shoulder bag. Pausing on the sidewalk in front of the café, she fished out the phone and pressed it to her ear. "Hello?"

"Bonjour, chérie." It was Luc. "I hope I am not interrupting your filming?"

"Good morning," Nicole said, a little surprised to hear from him again so soon. When Annike glanced over curiously, she mouthed Luc's name. "What are you up to today?" she asked him. "I thought you were working?"

"Indeed, today as always I must work," Luc replied. "However, tonight *je suis libre.* I was thinking of going to a holiday party at my favorite salsa club with a few people I know, and I am hoping that you and your friends can join me."

"Well, Patrice is definitely out—she's flying home this afternoon. But let me check with Annike." Nicole blocked the mouthpiece with her glove and told Annike what Luc had said.

"Salsa club?" Annike said. "Oh, yes! It sounds like fun."

"We're in," Nicole told Luc. "Where and when?"

She jotted down the directions Luc gave her, then hung

up and tucked both phone and directions back in her bag. When she looked up, Annike was grinning at her.

"What?" Nicole demanded.

"Your face went all pink and happy as soon as you heard it was Luc," Annike teased playfully. "Just as when we arrived at the bistro last night, Luc's face brightened as he saw you coming."

Nicole rolled her eyes. "Yeah, right. Luc looks at all the girls like that." She hoisted her bag farther up on her shoulder. "Now come on, let's get that coffee."

But as they walked back toward the Arc with their cups a few minutes later, Annike broached the subject again. "You do not have to pretend with me, Nicole," she said. "It is okay if being with Luc makes your heart go patter-pitter."

"It's pitter-patter," Nicole corrected, wrapping both hands around her cup to warm them. If possible, the morning had grown even rawer and chillier than it had been a few minutes earlier. "And it doesn't. I mean, yeah, it's good to see him again—just like it's good to see *you*. Or, you know, Paris. But Luc and I are friends now, that's all."

"Oh, yes?" Annike arched one perfectly groomed eyebrow.

"Yes," Nicole said firmly. "We're friends, and that's how it should be."

"But if he were to be interested in something more, and you were willing as well, then perhaps . . ."

"No way. I'm definitely not interested in spending my whole two weeks in Paris playing will-we-won't-we with Luc. So I'm telling you right now—we won't."

"All right." Annike looked slightly disappointed. "If you say so."

Nicole could tell that her friend wasn't really satisfied with her answer. She knew how that went. When someone was in love herself—as Annike was with Berg—she wanted everyone else to fall in love, too. But life didn't necessarily work that way. Sure, it would be easy enough to fall into the old patterns with Luc during this visit. But what would be the point when they only had two weeks together? Could any romance they might kindle for that short time be worth the risk of messing up their friendship over the long run? No, it made much more sense to spend these two weeks having fun—as friends—without the extra angst.

Soon after Nicole and Annike had returned to the group, the director finally called for attention. "All right, people," Nigel said, rubbing his hands together against the cold. "Here's how we're going to proceed this morning. We'd like to get a few group shots of you lot in front of the Arc. I want you to laugh, move about a bit—look as if you're having fun. All right? After that we'll move on to some individual interviews."

They all did as he said. But, the cameramen had been shooting for only a few minutes when Quinn let out a shout.

"Did anyone else feel that?" she said, holding up both hands, palms up. "It's raining!"

She was right. Within seconds, Nicole felt icy splatters on her face and saw the pavement going polka-dotted all around her.

"Oh, dear," Nigel said. "Cut! Quickly everyone, get under cover—let's see if it passes." As they all scooted toward the shelter of the Arc itself, Nicole heard the director add under his breath, "No such thing as a white Christmas in Paris, I'm afraid..."

Rather than passing, the rain only grew steadier and heavier over the next ten minutes. Nigel had been pacing back and forth and staring out at the weather, but finally he clapped his hands for attention.

"This is no use," he said. "We'll have to get back to this when the weather is better, perhaps later in the week. For now, why don't we head back to the S.A.S.S. building and do some interior work. There should be enough room for everyone in the vans if you're all willing to crowd in—follow me!"

A few minutes later Nicole found herself crushed into the back of a windowless van between Annike and a large piece of camera equipment that seemed to be almost entirely made up of sharp edges. Three of the French students were packed into their van as well, though Quinn, Yelena, and Claude had ended up in the second van.

"Wow," Nicole said as one of the cameramen slammed

the back door, leaving them in near darkness. "Talk about the glamorous life of a movie star!"

Annike giggled. "Yes. They seem to leave these bits out of the entertainment shows on TV4 back home."

The ride seemed to take forever, but finally the van pulled to a stop and someone came to release them. When Nicole climbed out, stretching to relieve her cramped muscles, she found herself in front of the S.A.S.S. building, an enormous, fortresslike stone structure that appeared to have stood in that very spot since time began. The flags of a dozen nations were flapping in the breeze overhead while stone lions stood sentry at the bottom of the steps.

"Look at that!" Annike squeezed Nicole's arm. "It looks just the same as it ever did, *non*?"

"Uh-huh." It was still raining, and Nicole didn't feel like standing there getting wet and cold, even to reminisce. "Come on, let's get inside." She hurried after the French students, who were already jogging up the broad steps toward the heavy wooden front doors.

The inside of the building looked much the same as well, other than the fact that the usual throngs of students were absent, the halls mostly deserted and echoing. As they wandered around the lobby, rubbing their hands to warm them up, Nicole and Annike immediately started reminiscing about shared friends and classes from their semester there.

After a moment Nigel hurried in, along with the stu-

dents from the second van. "Give us twenty minutes to set up, everyone!" the director called out. "Then meet us back here in the lobby and we can get started. There's another group already here, but we're going to take turns with the locations."

"Good." Annike checked her watch. "Twenty minutes—that gives me enough time to use the restroom. Want to come?"

"Sure." Nicole fell into step beside her friend as they headed away from the group and turned down one of the side hallways. When they reached the ladies' room, she waved Annike on. "Go ahead," she said. "I'll wait for you out here."

As Annike disappeared into the bathroom, Nicole leaned against the wall and glanced around the empty hallway. She was just a few doors down from her old French-language classroom. The culinary-arts lab was a little farther along the same hall, and just over there were the stairs leading upstairs to her Artist's Eye class...

Nicole was still staring toward that staircase when a guy appeared at the end of the hall. She blinked and focused on him. He was tall and broad-shouldered, with short sandy hair and a strong jaw. His ordinary blue jeans and striped T-shirt gave away nothing about his nationality.

Australian, maybe? Nicole guessed idly as the guy wandered closer. *Or he could be British, or German, or something like Polish...*

"Hi there."

Nicole belatedly realized that the guy was walking straight toward her now, a friendly smile on his face. "Oh!" she blurted out, a little embarrassed to be caught staring. "You—you're American!"

"So are you!" The guy sounded relieved. "Oh, man, it's good to hear that accent. Or nonaccent. Or—well, you know what I mean." He grinned and shrugged.

Nicole laughed. "Sure," she said. "I remember exactly what you mean. I studied here last year, and the first time I heard someone speaking in an American accent, I practically bowed down to kiss their feet. Oh! I'm Nicole, by the way. Nicole Larson, from Maryland."

"Mike Mooney." Mike stuck out his hand. "From Washington, D.C. What are the odds? We're practically neighbors!"

"I guess so." Nicole shook his hand. His grip was strong and hearty. "Are you here for the video filming?" She knew the students taking part in the project were divided into several groups each day, so she hadn't met all the others yet.

"Yeah, sort of." Mike swept a hand through his sandy hair. "I'm doing the S.A.S.S. program here in Paris next semester. They sent a letter asking if anyone could come a few weeks early and be in this video." He shrugged. "My folks are with the State Department, and they had to come to Europe for some conference this week. So I just

tagged along. They dropped me off here yesterday and continued on to Geneva. They're going to swing by again on Christmas Day before they head home." He glanced around. "In the meantime, I'm stuck here wondering why I can't understand a thing anyone says even after a year and a half of French class back home."

Just then Annike emerged from the restroom. Nicole introduced her to Mike. "He'll be in the program this coming semester," she explained.

"I see. So how are you finding your host family, Mike?" Annike asked. "Are they helping you to adjust to life in Paris?"

"Actually, I'm staying in this sort of dorm place for a few weeks," Mike said, his cheerful expression fading slightly. "My host family is away for the holidays—they'll be back right after New Year's."

"Oh, dear!" Annike looked sympathetic. "That must be a bit lonely, yes?"

Nicole nodded. It had been hard enough for her, arriving all alone in Paris with minimal language skills. But at least she'd had the Smiths waiting for her on the other end. She couldn't imagine how miserable she would have been if she'd been stuck there all by herself for the first several weeks.

"Hey, I have an idea," she said impulsively. "Annike and I are meeting a friend of ours tonight for some dinner and salsa dancing. Want to join us?"

"Really?" Mike's face lit up. "That would be awesome. Are you sure?"

"It is a wonderful idea!" Annike said. "Please, Mike. You must join us."

"Well, I have to check my book . . ." Mike grinned. "Just kidding. I'm totally there! Thanks!"

As the girls were making plans to meet him at the salsa club, the school's ancient PA system crackled to life. "Attention, please," Nigel's voice poured out of the nearest speaker. "Would the students with me today please report to the lobby immediately. Those in the group with Monsieur Reynolds, report to the auditorium. Thank you!"

"I'm in Reynolds's group," Mike said. "I'd better go."

"Us, too," Nicole said. "We're with Nigel. So I guess we'll see you tonight."

Mike smiled at her. "Can't wait."

Chapter Five

"I still can't believe I was such a jerk last night." Patrice leaned back against the scratchy black vinyl seat of the taxi, rolling her brown eyes up toward the ripped fabric of the ceiling. "I mean, getting loaded was one thing." She giggled and shot Nicole a look. "You already know I can't hold my alcohol!"

Nicole smiled at her. "I know."

Patrice's expression went serious again. "But then I had to go and flirt with your man..." she moaned.

"I keep telling you—he's not 'my man,'" Nicole said with a slightly exasperated sigh. "Luc is just a friend." *Why can't anyone seem to keep that straight?* she wondered, remembering Annike's comments earlier.

"Whatever." Patrice waved one hand. "I shouldn't have done it, and I'm totally sorry. Not to mention totally embarrassed."

"Forget about it." Nicole reached over and gave her knee a squeeze. "What's a little embarrassing behavior between friends? What happens in Paris stays in Paris."

She glanced out the window. The two girls had spent most of the ride talking about Nicole's day of filming, and Patrice's Christmas plans. Now they were almost at the airport. Checking her watch, Nicole saw that they had made good time from the city—Patrice had plenty of time to catch her flight.

"I can't believe you're leaving," she said. "It feels like you just got here!"

"It totally does," Patrice agreed. "But it also sort of feels like I've been in Europe for ages. Or maybe that's just the wine still messing up my brain!" She giggled.

"No, I know exactly what you mean," Nicole said. "It's like time is different here somehow. It's hard to explain."

The next few minutes were spent in a flurry of activity as they directed their driver to the right gate, unloaded Patrice's bags, and headed inside. But finally they found themselves walking toward the first security checkpoint.

Nicole stopped and turned to face her friend. "You'll have to go on by yourself from here," she said, swallowing

hard to stop the tears that suddenly seemed to be welling up behind her eyes. "I'm not allowed through security without a ticket."

"I know." Patrice dropped her bags, then flung herself at Nicole. "Oh my gosh, I'm going to miss you so much! I can't believe we won't see each other again for months and months!"

"I know," Nicole said, her voice muffled by Patrice's thick, dark hair. "But we'll e-mail. And I'll send you postcards, too, okay?"

"You'd better." Patrice pulled back and smiled at her. "And I especially want to hear all about your big night out dancing with Luc tonight."

"Okay," Nicole said, not bothering to remind her that her plans that evening weren't exactly the hot one-on-one date that she made it sound like.

"Listen, Nic. Luc is totally adorable, and obviously crazy about you." Patrice gazed at her, her expression suddenly going uncharacteristically serious. "I know you're a little gun-shy after the whole Nate thing. But I hope you won't hold that against Luc, you know?"

Nicole shrugged. "I'm not," she said. "But don't hold your breath for the wedding announcement, okay? I'm only here for two weeks, and I don't want to mess up my friendship with Luc by getting into anything complicated."

"Whatever." Patrice wasn't very good at hiding her feelings, and it was clear she thought Nicole was nuts not to go for it with Luc, limited time together or not. But she was a good enough friend not to say so. "Hey, then what about that Mike guy you met today?" she added hopefully. "Maybe you can see if there are any sparks there. He sounds cute!"

Nicole had told her a little about Mike along with everyone else she'd met at that day's filming. She laughed.

"You think anyone in pants sounds cute," she teased her friend fondly, pulling her in for another hug before fishing in her bag for her camera to take one last photo. "Face it, Patrice—you're just a hopeless romantic. But I'll miss you like crazy."

Nicole was still feeling a bit blue over her friend's departure as she and Annike pushed their way onto a crowded *métro* car that evening. They wedged themselves in between a harried-looking mother doing her best to hold on to three small children and a bunch of raucous German tourists wearing matching Santa Claus hats.

As the train lurched into motion, Annike shot Nicole a sympathetic glance. "Are you feeling sad that Patrice had to leave today?" she asked.

"Totally." Nicole smiled sheepishly. "It was really great having her here and showing her around Paris—it kind of made it even more fun, you know? Like getting to see it all through new eyes or something. Anyway, I miss her already. I wish she could've stayed longer."

Annike nodded. "I know. It's hard to say good-bye to someone you care about, isn't it? Even if you know you will see them again before too long."

"Are you thinking about saying good-bye to everyone back home if you decide to move to London for that show?" Nicole guessed, noticing the faraway look that had just come over her friend's face.

Annike chuckled. "Is it so obvious as that?" she asked, grabbing a pole for balance as the train car swayed. "Yes, you are correct. I cannot stop thinking about what it would be like, moving to a new city—a new country—without family or friends or even the S.A.S.S. program to keep me company. It all feels a bit grown-up and scary, you know? But I don't want to turn it down merely because I am afraid."

Nicole wasn't sure what to say. It was hard to imagine Annike being afraid of anything. She was always so confident and optimistic.

Just then the *métro* car came to a stop and the doors slid open. "Here is our stop, I think." Annike let go of the pole and joined the crush of people trying to all fit through the doors at once. "We don't want to miss it," she called back over her shoulder. "We were supposed to meet Luc five minutes ago!"

A few minutes later Nicole and Annike were approaching the salsa club. It was still drizzling and they were both wearing hooded raincoats over their cute dresses. When they got closer, Nicole spotted Mike standing on the sidewalk holding an umbrella and looking a bit forlorn as he watched the rain-soaked traffic go by. But his face lit up when he saw them.

"Thank goodness!" He hurried over and gallantly held the umbrella over them. "I still don't have the hang of finding my way around here. I was afraid I'd end up standing all night on the wrong street or something!"

The three of them entered the club and found Luc waiting for them in the lobby. *"Bonsoir."* He greeted Nicole and Annike with his usual hug and double-barreled kiss. He took in their festive outfits and smiled. "You both look even more beautiful than usual, if such a thing is possible." Then he glanced curiously at Mike, who was hovering behind the girls doing his best to fold up his umbrella without dripping water all over the place. "And who have we here?"

"This is Mike," Nicole said. "He just arrived in Paris for next semester's S.A.S.S. program."

"I'm doing that video thing with these two," Mike added, shaking Luc's hand. "Nicole and Annike found me wandering around all alone and pathetic, so they took pity and invited me to tag along with you guys tonight. Hope you don't mind, man."

"Not at all," Luc said. "*Plus on est des fous, plus on rit.* Come, I have secured us a table inside."

With Luc in the lead, they all pushed through another

set of doors into the main part of the club. A swinging Christmas party was going on in there; people were crowded around the dozen or so round tables clustered at the near end of the room. At the center of each table was a candle tucked into a holiday wreath, and swags of holly and other greenery decorated the walls. The other half of the place was taken up by a dance floor splattered with droplets of swirling light from the large disco ball overhead. There was nobody out there at the moment, though a jazzy, spicy version of "O Tannenbaum" was pouring out of the speakers.

Luc led them to a table off to one side bordering the dance floor. Half a dozen people were already seated there—a pair of cute, well-dressed guys around Luc's age, along with four pretty girls.

"Here we are," Luc said, raising his voice to be heard above the music. "Our table. Please, be seated, everyone. I shall make introductions now, *oui*?"

He introduced them to his friends, who all seemed friendly enough, though several of them spoke very little English. While Mike and Annike were busy finding an extra chair—there were only three empty ones left at the table when they arrived—Luc pulled out a seat for Nicole and gestured for her to sit down. When she did, he leaned over to push her chair in, speaking softly into her ear as he did so.

"*Je suis au bout du rouleau,* Nicole," he said, putting a

playful pout in his voice. "Shall I be jealous of your handsome new American friend? He seems very fond of you."

Nicole glanced up at him and laughed. "I can't tell you how to feel, my friend," she joked back.

Luc stepped back and put one hand over his heart, looking pained. But his eyes were twinkling with fun.

Nicole laughed again. Some things never changed!

Over a dinner of spicy, flavorful Spanish food, the group chatted about Christmas, S.A.S.S., and Paris while a couple of Luc's friends practiced their English—and one of the guys returned the favor by teaching the Americans and Annike some colorful French swearwords. Nicole was happy to note that Mike turned out to be just as smart and outgoing as he'd seemed on their first meeting; he had the whole table laughing within minutes with his vivid description of trying to do some last-minute Christmas shopping at an overcrowded Virginia mall. Despite his all-American accent and humble comments on his own language skills, Nicole realized he was actually more savvy about the world than she'd first assumed.

I guess having parents who work for the State Department will do that for you, she thought, gazing at him thoughtfully as she took a sip of her drink. She couldn't help feeling intrigued.

Once the waiters started clearing away the dessert plates, it wasn't long before the dancing started. A live band had come in and set up while they were eating, and

during the end of the dessert course they launched into the first of a series of spirited salsa numbers. Before long Nicole's toes were tapping under the table, and her shoulders were moving in time to the music.

"They are very good, are they not?" Annike said into her ear.

Nicole nodded, watching admiringly as several couples swept onto the dance floor and started spinning each other around. "I've never tried salsa dancing," she called back. "But it looks like fun!"

Luc heard her and leaned over. "Ah, but it *is* fun, *chérie*." He held out his hand. "Shall I give you a lesson on how it is done?"

Nicole hesitated only briefly before placing her hand in his and allowing him to lead her out onto the floor. *Friends are allowed to dance, right?* she thought, shrugging off a flutter of nervousness. *And I'm supposed to be all about trying new things this year. Salsa dancing certainly seems to qualify!*

Luc showed Nicole a few steps, and between that and watching the other couples, she was soon doing a passable job at salsa dancing. Luc was a good partner, guiding her with a featherlight touch through the steps, his own movements fluid and sure.

"This is fun," Nicole said breathlessly as they paused between songs. "You know, it seems kind of weird that we've never danced together before. You're really good!"

The band struck up another number, this one a bit slower and sultrier than the last. Luc pulled her toward him again. One of his arms wrapped around her waist, and the other hand squeezed hers tightly, bringing her closer until their bodies touched.

"It is true, we have not danced in a club like we are doing now," he said in a low voice. "But we have danced together, Nicole, you and I. We had one dance at Versailles, *oui*? And another one evening while we looked up at La Tour Eiffel..."

Nicole bit her lip, realizing he was referring to the times they'd kissed. She was glad that his head was turned so he couldn't see the emotions playing out on her face. Suddenly things were feeling a little less friendly and a lot more romantic than they had just a moment ago. She was very aware of his arms holding her close, the scent of his aftershave, the feel of his chest moving against hers with each breath...

She closed her eyes, suddenly overwhelmed with the memory of those kisses. *What if I turned my head toward him right now?* a little voice inside her wondered. *Would he kiss me again, right here in the middle of the dance floor? And if he did... then what?*

Before she could figure out what to do about the confusing emotions welling up inside her, she saw Mike weaving his way through the couples toward them. A second later he was tapping Luc on the shoulder.

"Sorry to cut in, buddy," he said with a grin. "But your friend Alain already asked Annike to dance, and the other girls got snapped up, too. And I can't wait any longer to try this salsa thing. Mind if I steal Nicole for a song or two?"

Luc immediately loosened his hold on Nicole and stepped back. "But of course," he said with a bow of his head. "Be my guest, *je vous en prie*."

Nicole glanced at him, both disappointed and relieved to have that intense moment interrupted. Had his face and voice held a shadow of annoyance at Mike's arrival? Or was that only her imagination?

Luc was already wending his way off across the floor. Nicole couldn't help noticing that he wasn't heading back to their table, but rather aiming straight toward one of the French girls from their group who was standing with several other cute young women over near the wall watching the dancers.

"Shall we?" Mike said, holding out his arms.

Nicole snapped out of her reverie. "Sure."

They began to dance, though there was quite a bit more space between them than there had been between her and Luc. Mike wasn't nearly as lithe and graceful as Luc, though he moved pretty well for such a big guy.

Seeming to read her mind, he smiled. "I hope I don't step on you or anybody else," he joked. "My buddies and I don't do too much salsa dancing back home."

"Me, either." Nicole smiled at him, trying not to notice

Luc leading a pretty brunette in a very short skirt onto the floor a short distance away. This friends-only thing was getting tricky already…

She tried to shake off such thoughts. This would be a problem only if she let it be. Sure, Luc was being flirty and romantic. But that was just Luc. He had been that way pretty much since the first time she'd met him last year. If she wanted to have a nice, friendly time with him during this visit, all she had to do was what she'd done then—stay vigilant against his advances, and be very careful to keep things casual.

As the song ended and a new one began, she pushed all thoughts of Luc aside and focused on Mike. The two of them talked as they danced. It was amazing how much they had in common. Although their homes were some thirty or forty miles apart, Nicole and her high school friends had made the trip to D.C. fairly often. So she and Mike knew a lot of the same places and had done a lot of the same things.

"You know, I'm totally glad I ran into you and Annike yesterday," Mike said as the current song faded away and the band prepared to start their next number. "You've really made me feel much more at home on my first day all alone in Paris."

Nicole smiled up at him. "Glad I could help," she said. "I remember how that felt."

He reached over and squeezed her arm. "Thanks." He

hesitated, then smiled. "So how about helping me settle in even more by having dinner with me tomorrow night? Just the two of us, I mean."

Nicole gulped, realizing he was asking her out on a date. "Um, I don't know," she said. "You're really cool, but I'm not sure that's such a good idea. I mean, I'm only here for a couple of weeks, and..."

"Oh, no, that's okay." Mike shot a glance at Luc, who was laughing and chatting with his dance partner nearby during the break in the music. "Sorry, my bad. I didn't realize you and Luc were, you know, together."

"We're not," Nicole said quickly. "Um, it's just kind of bad timing, you know? It's nothing to do with Luc—or you, either. Honestly."

He looked disappointed but shrugged and smiled good-naturedly. "Okay, consider me let down easy," he said. "I hope I didn't just make things weird between us by asking you out—I mean, you're still one of my only friends in Paris so far!"

She couldn't help laughing. Mike might not be as smooth and sophisticated as Luc, but he really *was* sort of charming in his own understated way.

"Nope, we're cool," she assured him just as the band started up its next song. Spotting Annike passing by on her own, she waved her over. "But I think I'll let Annike cut in for this dance," she told Mike with a smile. "I need a drink of water."

Annike had reached them just in time to hear her. She looked a bit confused but nodded agreeably.

"Shall we dance, *monsieur*?" she asked Mike.

"I'd be honored."

Nicole left the two of them salsaing together and made her way off the crowded dance floor. It was very warm in the club, and she really was thirsty.

But more than that, she wanted to get away by herself for a moment. Mike's invitation had taken her by surprise, and she was already wondering if she should have been so quick to turn him down. He seemed like a really great guy, and just her type. Then again, there were a lot of great guys in the world. Did she really want to spend this two weeks in Paris with Mike if it meant giving up some of her time with the friends she'd come back to see? She wasn't sure what to think. When she'd invited Mike along tonight, she'd never imagined things could get complicated with him so quickly.

She glanced back over her shoulder, searching for Luc, though she couldn't find him in the mass of dancers. *And I'm thinking more complication is exactly what I* don't *need right now,* she thought with a sigh.

From: PatriceQT@email.com

To: NicLar@email.com

Subject: home boring home

Hey Nic,

Just lettin u know I made it back to the US of A alive. (tho barely—that airplane food is BLECH!!!)

NEway, I had a totally aWeSoMe time w/u in Italy & France! Europe is even cooler than u made it sound, lol. Makes me think I should look in2 the study abroad pro-

> gram here at the uni. What do u think?
>
> O, & then there's monsieur Luc—he's way hotter than u made him sound, 2! W/a guy like that pining 4 u in Paris, I can't blieve u ever actually came back here!!! lol lol lol (but I'm totally not kidding!!!!!!) U better let me know what happens w/u 2!
>
> Miss ya already sweetie!
>
> P.

The next day dawned as wet and dreary as the one before. Nicole yawned and stared out at the rain. She and Annike were huddled beneath a too-small umbrella near yet another wet Parisian landmark—this time Notre Dame cathedral. Rain dripped off its Gothic arches and buttresses and the branches of the huge, lavishly decorated Christmas tree that stood in the courtyard outside the front doors, forming puddles that reflected back the twinkling holiday lights that seemed to drape the entire city these days. Across the plaza, Nigel was consulting with the cameramen, who had draped plastic cloths over most of their equipment.

"Another exciting day in showbiz," Nicole commented.

Annike took a sip of her coffee, gazing up at the rain-spattered façade of the famous cathedral. "At least we got some footage earlier when the rain stopped for a moment."

"Always looking on the bright side, aren't you?" Nicole

asked her with a chuckle. "You actually seem to be enjoying all this hurry-up-and-wait!"

Annike smiled. "It would be better out of the rain, *ja,* but it has been enjoyable."

"I bet the filming for your show will be much more fun; it probably takes place indoors!"

At that moment the rain slowed a bit and the director called for attention. "Okay, let's see if we can get something done here!" he called out. "We're going to take our multilingual Christmas carol from the top."

"Oh, man," Nicole muttered to Annike with a giggle. "If I never hear 'Jingle Bells' again—in any language—it will be too soon."

The idea for today's first filming session was to have the students stand in front of Notre Dame singing "Jingle Bells" in various languages to play up the seasonal aspect of the new Wintermission program. All over the city, Nigel and the other two directors involved in the project would repeat the exercise at other famous sites while the directors in the other cities would do the same. In the end, the footage would be spliced into one big number, jumping from language to language with every line. Nicole was sure the end result would be pretty cool, but making it was turning out to be awfully boring. They'd spent the first half hour of rain in the van practicing the lyrics in their different languages.

"You two"—Nigel pointed to Sylvie and Claude, the

French students—"you start us off on the chorus *en français,* all right? Then for the second line, I want Sylvie to continue on in Japanese, and then Hamadi can pick it up in Arabic." He pointed to the fifth member of the group, one of Mike's fellow S.A.S.S. Paris program newcomers, who hailed from Cairo. "Then Nicole, Claude, and Annike can finish us off in English. We'll do the Swedish and Spanish lines on the next take. Got it?"

Nicole lowered the umbrella. It was still spitting a little, but not too much. "Okay," she said to Annike with a sigh. "Let's go jingle our little hearts out."

They had only managed to get about ten more minutes' worth of footage when the clouds opened up again, chasing them all into the shelter of the cathedral's entrance. Nigel peered out at the driving rain splashing off the ground and churning the waters of the Seine and groaned.

Nicole knew how he felt. It wasn't just wet, it was cold, too. Despite her warm coat and gloves, she was starting to shiver.

"This is rubbish," the director muttered, pulling out his cell phone and making a call. When he hung up, he called for everyone to gather around. "We're going to give up on the outdoor shots for now and join one of the other groups that's shooting indoors today. Back to the vans, everyone!"

A short while later they were all walking into the soaring

atrium of the Musée d'Orsay, the well-known art museum housed in a converted railway station. "Awesome," Nicole said as she peeled off her wet coat. "This is one of my favorite places in Paris!"

"Mine, too," Annike agreed. "Look, there's the other group." Nicole looked where her friend was pointing and saw several familiar faces gathered near one of the sculptures in the main hall. The group they were joining included Mike, Quinn, and Yelena.

Nigel had already hurried ahead to consult with the other director, a brisk young French woman named Félice. By the time Nicole and Annike had joined the group and exchanged greetings with the other students, the directors had concocted a plan.

"Listen up, please," Félice said. Her voice wasn't loud, but it carried and made everyone pay attention, including a group of curious-looking Asian tourists who happened to be passing by at the moment. "We are going to do some candid shooting now. I want you to all sit on those benches over there"—she paused just long enough to point with one manicured finger—"and have a conversation with one another about your experiences with art and culture during your time abroad. Those of you who are new to the program shall listen and ask questions of the others. We shall film you all talking, but I want you to pretend the cameras are not here, *oui*?"

"Yeah, right," Nicole whispered to Annike as they

made their way toward the benches with the others. "Just pretend you don't remember this is going to be seen by people all over the world every time they visit the S.A.S.S. Web site, *oui*?"

Annike smiled but didn't answer. Nicole wondered if she was thinking about that reality show again. Before she could ask, Mike caught up to them.

"Hey, what happened?" he asked. "We heard you guys were over at Notre Dame today."

"We were." Nicole ran her hand through her hair, which was still damp. "We got rained out. So we decided to crash your party."

Mike laughed a little harder than the lame comment deserved. But before he could say anything else, the directors called for attention again. Nicole found a seat between Annike and Hamadi, and Mike sat down on the next bench with Claude and Quinn. Then they got started.

For the first few minutes, despite Félice's orders, Nicole couldn't help feeling self-conscious about being filmed. But several of the others, including Annike, seemed to have no such qualms. Before long they were involved in a lively discussion about the art, architecture, and other cultural offerings of Paris and the other cities they'd visited. Nicole found herself caught up in the conversation before she knew it, and even managed to add a few intelligent comments of her own.

The only thing marring the pleasant exchange was

Quinn. At first the British girl had been fairly quiet. But when Yelena timidly spoke up to mention that one of her favorite things about Paris was its food, Quinn practically jumped down the Russian girl's throat, insisting that food didn't count as "culture."

The others tactfully changed the subject, and Yelena didn't seem overly affected—she continued to put in her soft-spoken comments here and there. But the incident left Nicole feeling cranky, especially when Quinn interrupted Annike in the middle of her comparison of the architecture of Stockholm to that of Paris.

Nicole managed to shrug off such feelings after a while when the talk turned to the museums of Paris. Mike had started it off by asking everyone what their favorite was. After several of the others had put in their opinions that the Louvre and/or the d'Orsay were the best, Nicole spoke up.

"I totally adore this place, too," she said. "And of course the Louvre is the Louvre. But I think my personal favorite might be the Georges Pompidou Center. It's just so—different." She smiled, remembering how Luc had introduced her to the unusual modern-art museum with its playful sculpture fountain. That had been a special day—one of the first times she'd suspected she and Luc might become real friends.

"What?" Quinn laughed derisively. "You're having us on, right? Who could choose that monstrosity over this gorgeous place?" She waved a hand at the lovely museum around them.

Nicole drew back, feeling as if she'd been slapped. "Well, okay," she said. "I didn't say it was the most *beautiful* building in Paris. But nobody had mentioned it yet, and it *is* a pretty important museum..."

"I enjoy the Pompidou Center as well," Sylvie spoke up. "Did you know the architecture was the result of a design contest back in the 1970s...?"

The rest of the group continued talking, but Nicole wasn't really paying attention. She was stewing over what had just happened. Why had she backed down like that when Quinn had attacked her choice?

I know why, she thought grimly, sneaking a glance at the British girl. *Habit. Years of habit. I thought now that high school is over, I would be better at standing up for myself. But maybe it's not that easy.*

"It is not fair!" Annike cried breathlessly. "No sooner had we dried off than we had to go back out into the rain again!"

She and Nicole had just raced up the steps to their flat. The sky had appeared to be clearing when they'd been dismissed from the day's shooting, which had almost made Nigel and Félice rethink their decision to knock off early. But that decision had proved to be a good one when

Nicole and Annike had emerged from their home *métro* station just in time to get soaked anew by yet another cloudburst.

"I know," Nicole agreed, standing back as her friend unlocked the door. "But that's what hot showers are for. I call first dibs!"

"Dibs?" Annike repeated, swinging open the door. "What is dibs? Oh, look—there is my phone!"

She had forgotten to bring her cell with them that day. Now she hurried into the apartment and retrieved it from the coffee table. She sat down on the sofa and peered at it.

"Did Hollywood call?" Nicole shrugged off her coat and hung it by the door.

"No, but someone did. My parents—they ask me to call them back." Annike punched a button on the phone and put it to her ear. When someone answered on the other end, she started talking in Swedish.

Nicole kicked off her shoes and checked her watch. It was so gloomy outside from all the rain that it seemed much later than it was. In fact, it was barely 2 P.M. Her stomach rumbled as she realized she hadn't had lunch.

She walked over to the minuscule fridge in the tiny kitchenette and took out an Orangina, surveying the other contents for food ideas. When she turned around again, Annike was just hanging up, a slight frown clouding her usual sunny expression.

"What did your folks want?" Nicole asked when her

friend turned off the phone. "Is everything okay?"

Annike sighed, looking guilty. "Yes, everything is fine," she said. "It seems my grades have arrived from the past semester at university."

"Uh-oh. Bad news?"

"No, I did very well."

Nicole took a sip of her drink, feeling a bit confused. "That's great," she said. "So why do you look so upset?"

Annike stood up and started pacing back and forth across the tiny room. "That is just it," she exclaimed. "How can I tell them I might not be going back to school? It will break their hearts!"

"Oh." Nicole bit her lip, feeling helpless. She hated seeing Annike so uncertain. "Well, your parents may think your education is super important, but I'm sure most of all they want you to be happy. They'll understand, no matter what you decide."

"I suppose so." Annike stopped pacing. "In any case, it will all be decided one way or another soon enough." She smiled wryly. "I only wish I knew what that decision would be."

Just then Nicole's phone rang. She grabbed it out of her bag and answered. It was Mike.

"I was just calling to see what's up," he said. "What did you think of today's filming? Pretty interesting, huh?"

"Sure." Nicole was a little distracted as she watched Annike wander over to look in the fridge. "Today was cool."

"Yeah." Mike let out a snort. "Well, except for that Quinn girl, anyway. How do you say *obnoxious* in French? Because that girl should be in some kind of international dictionary."

That got Nicole's attention. "Oh my God, yes!" she exclaimed. She'd wanted to complain about Quinn on the way home but had held back. Annike didn't seem overly impressed with the loud British girl, either, but then again, Annike always tried hard to see the best in people. Nicole hadn't wanted to sound too petty. "I was ready to kill her when she was so rude to Yelena."

"I know. Yelena's great—she may be quiet, but the girl is sharp, know what I mean? I don't know why she puts up with all Quinn's crap."

"Well, they're rooming together." Nicole switched the phone to her other ear as she sat down on the sofa. "Maybe she's just trying to keep the peace."

"Maybe. But I'll tell you, Quinn was really pissing me off." Mike hesitated before going on. "Actually, I was probably overreacting, though. See, my brother Bill is always riding me like that. He's three years older, and he seems to think that means he can boss me around about everything."

"Really?" Nicole was surprised. Mike seemed so easy-going and confident that it was hard to believe anyone else could ever get to him. "Well, now that you mention it, I used to have this friend named Zara . . ." Before she quite realized it, she found herself giving him the Cliff's Notes version of her high school years. Annike glanced over at her once or twice in surprise before wandering off into the bedroom.

"Whoa," Mike said when Nicole finished. "I never would have guessed! You seem so sure of yourself now. Totally not the type of person who'd let anyone else tell her what to do."

"Thanks." Nicole found herself smiling into the phone. Mike was right—she *wasn't* that girl anymore. "You know, I was kind of bummed about not standing up to Quinn today, actually. But talking to you is making me feel better."

"Really? How about paying me back by changing your mind about having dinner with me tonight in Montmartre?"

Nicole could tell he was half joking, but even so, she couldn't help giving in to impulse for once. After all, what was the harm in one little dinner? "Okay, it's a deal," she said. "But just as friends, right?"

"Sure, good enough." Mike sounded surprised but pleased. "It's a date!"

Chapter Seven

Nicole was too hungry to wait any longer for lunch, so she let Annike have the shower first after all while she wolfed down an orange and a cheese sandwich. She was just finishing a granola bar she'd found in her suitcase when Annike emerged wrapped in a terry-cloth robe, looking pink-cheeked and refreshed.

"It is all yours," she said. "I can dry my hair out here."

"Thanks." Nicole grabbed her things and hurried into the bathroom. Like the rest of the apartment, it was tiny. There was barely enough room for the ancient, chipped toilet and pedestal sink along with the vinyl-encased shower stall. Both the cracked mirror above the sink and the narrow, barred window overlooking an alley were steamed over after Annike's shower.

After peeling off her clothes and draping them across the sink, Nicole stepped into the shower stall and turned on the water as hot as she could stand it. She closed her eyes and stood under the spray for a long time, letting the steamy water wash away the chill of the damp December day along with her worries and frustrations.

Finally she climbed out and wrapped herself in a fluffy bath towel, feeling not only cleaner and warmer but also much more relaxed than when she'd started. Why stress so much over some obnoxious comments by someone she'd probably never see again after next week? Not to mention her anxiety over Luc and now a few second thoughts over whether she should have agreed to tonight's date with Mike. What was that French expression?

"Qué sera, sera," she whispered. "Whatever will be, will be."

Still wearing only her towel, she went out into the main room, where Annike was sitting at the tiny dining table reading *Le Monde* and drinking a cup of instant coffee. She was fully dressed by now and glanced up when Nicole entered.

"It seems to have stopped raining again," she said,

gesturing toward the windows. "I was thinking of doing a little shopping. Would you like to join me? I can wait while you get dressed."

"No, that's okay," Nicole said. "Are you taking your cell? Maybe I'll call you and meet up with you later." She smiled sheepishly. "I'm feeling too lazy and relaxed to hurry right now."

"It is all right. I understand that feeling." Annike took her coffee cup to the sink and pulled on her coat. "I'll see you later, then."

"Bye."

After Annike had gone, Nicole quickly blow-dried her hair and then padded around the apartment in her towel trying to decide what clothes to put on and what to do for the rest of the day before it was time to meet Mike for dinner. Annike's comment about shopping had reminded her that she still hadn't decided what to do about Christmas gifts for her friends, and she wondered if she should use the time to do a little shopping herself.

Before she could figure it out, there was a knock on the apartment door. Nicole smiled and hurried over, figuring it had to be Annike.

"That was quick," she called as she undid the lock. "Did you forget your key, or..."

Her voice drifted off in midsentence as the door swung open. It wasn't Annike on the other side after all. It was Luc.

"Oh." Nicole blushed, suddenly uncomfortably aware that she was standing there wearing only a towel. "Um, hi."

"Bonjour." Luc looked casually gorgeous in a wool sweater and an unbuttoned black jacket. His expression was both amused and appreciative as his gaze wandered down her body. "*Tu as bonne mine.* I am glad to see you did not bother to dress up for my visit. May I come in?"

"Um, sure." Nicole stepped back, grabbing at the top of the towel to make sure it didn't slip. Her face was flaming and she didn't dare meet Luc's eye.

"Excuse me," she muttered. "I'll be right back."

Leaving him to shut the apartment door behind him, she scurried into the bedroom, closed the door, and collapsed against it. *Nice way to make sure to keep things on a strictly friendship level between Luc and me,* she thought ruefully. *Greet him at the door half naked—that'll do the trick...*

Taking a few deep breaths, she did her best to compose herself as she grabbed some clothes and pulled them on. Then, after making certain that all of her buttons were buttoned and her zippers zipped, she opened the door and went back out to the main room. Luc was standing by the windows looking out, but he turned around and surveyed her when she entered.

"Seems I had caught you at a bad time," he said with a twinkle in his eye.

"What are you doing here?" Nicole asked, willing herself

not to blush again. "Um, I mean, I wasn't expecting you."

"I am sorry to surprise you." Luc didn't sound sorry at all as he walked across the room toward her. "I unexpectedly have the afternoon off from babysitting and thought I would take the opportunity to view the Christmas window decorations at Galeries Lafayette and Printemps. It is one of my favorite Parisian traditions. And there is no one I would rather share it with this year than my favorite American girl. What do you say?"

"Um..." she began, not sure how to respond. Somehow, the apartment felt even smaller than usual with Luc in it, as if the walls were closing in around the two of them.

He took a step closer, still smiling. Nicole realized her heart was pounding. Even though she was fully dressed now, she still felt weirdly exposed. Maybe it was the way he was looking at her...

She was having a lot of trouble ignoring the sparks she felt flying between Luc and herself. Based on the expression in his eyes, he was completely aware of those sparks, too.

"Those Christmas windows sound good," she blurted out, jumping back so quickly that she almost tripped over the coffee table. "Let's go check them out."

"Wow, the lighting in this one is so dramatic and beautiful!" Nicole said, gazing at the glittering holiday presentation in the window of Paris's celebrated Printemps department store. The entire façade of the massive building was decked out in colorful lights and huge snowflakes, and each window mixed edgy high fashion and charming holiday touches. She shoved both hands into her coat pockets and shivered. After all the rain, it had turned into a pleasant but chilly afternoon.

"Are you cold?" Luc asked. "Come, why don't we go inside the store to warm up."

"Good idea." Nicole turned and followed as he headed toward the store's entrance. Once she'd recovered from the awkward start to her afternoon with Luc, she'd actually started having a nice time. They had taken the *métro* to the ninth *arrondissement* and then spent a couple of hours strolling up and down Boulevard Haussmann and nearby streets looking at the window displays and other holiday decorations, stopping off occasionally to browse in a shop or have a coffee at a bistro whenever they got chilled. With every passing day the city seemed more steeped in the Christmas spirit. Today the holiday lights were already twinkling, pale but cheerful against the rapidly fading daylight, and the atmosphere on the streets was festive and friendly, making the large, bustling city feel much more intimate somehow. Nicole had been so busy finishing her semester and preparing to return to the United States the previous year that she hadn't had a chance to stop and appreciate any of that, which made her enjoy the atmosphere all the more now.

She was also enjoying the company. Luc was in an especially relaxed mood that made him very easy to hang out with. As they'd strolled along, they had chatted about anything and everything—the holidays, their families, Nicole's European travels, Luc's jobs, shared friends, and more.

"So, how's school going?" Nicole asked as the department store's main door opened to admit them with a puff of heated air that felt like a warm breath on their faces. She took her hands out of her pockets and rubbed them together, then unzipped her jacket. "You mentioned you'd probably have your degree finished sometime next fall. What then?"

Luc shot her a quick look, and for a moment Nicole expected him to respond with a quip or some obscure French philosophical quote about living in the moment, and then immediately change the subject. Instead he shrugged.

"I do not know," he said. "Such questions have been occupying my thoughts a great deal lately."

"Really?" Nicole felt a rush of kinship with him. As much as she was enjoying her adventures traveling around Europe, it sometimes felt as if she was the only one who didn't know where she would be a year from now. After a lifetime spent trying to plan and control everything, that feeling was kind of scary sometimes. "Well, with a degree in business, I suppose you'll have lots of options."

"Oui." He shrugged again. "My mother, she expects me to become involved in the financial world and make a lot of money. And yet, when I think of that, I am not sure it is for me, *tu sais ce que je veux dire*?"

"Yeah, I know exactly what you mean." Nicole smiled at him. "What do you think you want to do instead?"

"Ah, who knows. Even with the many hours I work now, I enjoy how different every day is. Some days I am waiting tables and flirting with the girls at the restaurant, some days I am proofreading in the park, some days I am at class and then babysitting. I should not like to be working in finance and stuck behind the same desk every single day."

Nicole nodded. After all the traveling she'd been doing, it was tough to imagine herself in that role, either.

"I think I would like to be out doing something with people. To use my degree to help in some way." Luc sighed. "I do not know. In any case, it is much too dreary a subject for such a pleasant day." He shrugged again, turning away to gesture at the store around them. "What about this place, eh? I am told that all American girls adore shopping—is it true, *chérie*?" He leered playfully at her, all traces of his earlier vulnerability gone as if they'd never been there at all.

Nicole couldn't help being a bit disappointed at the abrupt change in subject and mood. Still, she was amazed—and perhaps a little flattered?—that he'd opened up so much to her just now.

"I can't believe I've never been in here before," she commented as she glanced around at the seemingly endless displays of luxurious merchandise surrounding them on the department store's main floor. "I must have passed it a million times last year, but I never came in."

Luc chuckled. "Ah, *oui.*" He glanced over at her as they wandered down the main aisle. "But what is that English expression? Better late than never?"

His words held a hint of flirtation, but Nicole chose to ignore it. They were having such a fun, friendly time—why spoil that?

"Speaking of buying stuff," she said, "I've barely started my Christmas shopping and I'm starting to panic. You've met Patrice now, and of course you know Annike. What do you think I should get them?"

The distraction worked. They spent the next half hour or so discussing the possibilities. After glancing at a few price tags, Nicole quickly decided that she wouldn't be doing any of her shopping at Printemps—not on her tight budget! Still, she couldn't resist looking around. After all, window shopping was free—even at the renowned, luxurious, architecturally stunning Printemps!

"Too bad Patrice isn't still here." By now they were browsing through a display of home furnishings on one of the store's upper levels. "She loves shopping—she'd totally adore this place."

"Mademoiselle Patrice was charming indeed," Luc said. "But I cannot agree that I wish she were here with us now. If so, I would have to share your attention with her, and that would be something I would not like. Not at all."

Nicole glanced over and saw Luc gazing back with a smile. Turning away to finger a tablecloth in a display nearby, she willed herself not to blush. How was it that he could manage to throw her off balance with just a few words and that certain look in his green eyes?

"Well, anyway, I'll have to e-mail her and let her know what she missed." Nicole covered her flustered feelings by digging into her bag for her camera. She snapped a few photos of the store, then glanced over at Luc. He was still gazing at her with that amused expression.

"Ready to go?" he asked. "The hour is getting late, and I'm feeling hungry. I know of a lovely bistro not far from here where we should be able to get a *very* private table in the back, if you would care to—"

"Oh my gosh!" Nicole gasped, interrupting him. She had just glanced at her watch. "I totally lost track of the time! I'm going to be so late—I'm supposed to be at that Indian place up in Montmartre in like twenty minutes!"

"Say no more." Luc was immediately all business. "Come, all hope is not lost—with a bit of luck, I shall have you there *à l'heure*."

Nicole followed as he rushed for the stairs, hoping he

was right. She hated the thought of leaving poor Mike standing out in the cold in an unfamiliar part of the city. She thought about trying to reach him on his cell to let him know she was running late but decided not to waste the time. She already knew from her previous visit that Luc had lived in Paris all his life and was an absolute master at finding his way around. If anyone could get her there on time, it was him.

They hurried out of the store and then sprinted down the street to the *métro* station, reaching the platform just as a train was arriving. If Nicole had been making the trip alone, she still would have been poring over the map trying to figure out which way to go, and she felt a flash of gratitude as Luc grabbed her hand and helped her push her way on board.

Once they emerged at the other end, Luc continued to lead the way. He knew all the shortcuts there were, and by three minutes to seven they were skidding to a stop in front of the restaurant in question.

"Wow, thanks!" Nicole said breathlessly, pushing back the sleeve of her jacket to check her watch. "I can't believe we actually made it!"

He made a playful little half bow. "It is my pleasure to help you in any way required, *chérie*," he said. "Although if you wished to express your thanks by inviting me to join you for dinner, it is I who would be in your debt."

Nicole blinked, a bit taken aback. She couldn't believe that Luc was inviting himself along on her dinner date with Mike. That seemed pretty forward, even for Luc…

"That is," Luc went on, "unless you and the lovely Annike were intending to—"

Nicole's heart sank; she realized her mistake at the same moment a cheerful voice called out her name. Glancing over her shoulder, she saw Mike hurrying down the sidewalk toward them, looking broad-shouldered and handsome in a dark peacoat.

Luc saw him, too. "Oh, I see," he murmured as Mike approached.

"I can't believe I made it," Mike said breathlessly. "That *métro* map is so confusing I was afraid I'd be—Oh." He stopped and stared at Luc, obviously surprised and perhaps a bit wary. "Um, hello, Luc. Nice to see you again."

"And you as well." Luc nodded politely. "I was just leaving. Enjoy your dinner."

"Luc, wait," Nicole began, feeling terrible. She hadn't meant to mislead him. In her panic when she'd noticed the time, she now realized that she hadn't specified who it was she was supposed to be meeting; Luc had clearly assumed it was Annike. And why shouldn't he?

But Luc had already disappeared into the crowds rushing past in both directions. Mike shrugged, not looking too sorry to see him go.

"Shall we?" he asked, offering his arm to Nicole.

She smiled weakly and nodded. "We shall."

Nicole wasn't sure what she'd been expecting from her dinner with Mike, especially after its rather awkward start, but she was kind of amazed by just how comfortable it felt to hang out with him—almost as if they'd known each other much longer than just a couple of days. He was easy to talk to, and the more talking they did, the more they discovered they had in common.

"I'm really glad I decided to come over to Paris early," Mike said, smiling at her across the table. "I wasn't sure at first—you know, I didn't want to miss the Christmas parties at home or whatever."

Nicole nodded and speared a bite of tandoori chicken with her fork. "I know what you mean. When I first came over here last year, I couldn't stop thinking about all the stuff I was missing back home. But it turned out I didn't miss all that much, really. At least nothing important."

"I feel like these two extra weeks are giving me a head start," Mike said. "My French is getting way better already, for one thing."

"You're lucky." Nicole sat back as a waiter materialized to refill her glass. "I didn't speak a word when I got here."

Mike shot her an admiring glance. "That's amazing to me," he said. "It's one thing to move to another country. But one where you don't speak the language?" He shrugged. "I'm not that brave!"

"Trust me, I'm not, either," Nicole said with a smile. "My parents practically had to tie me up and force me on the plane to get here!"

"Okay, but look at you now." Mike stirred his rice. "You've been traveling all over to places where you don't know the languages, all on your own. And that was your idea, right?" He pointed his fork at her. "Face it, dude—you're brave."

Nicole laughed. "Okay, maybe you're right. I'm a total Amazon woman," she joked.

Mike grinned at her, then turned his attention to his food. "Actually, I'm feeling kind of brave for ordering this spicy food you recommended," he said. "Not to mention figuring out the *métro*, learning to salsa dance, seeing all the cool stuff they've been filming us in front of..."

"See? You're a rock star, too," Nicole joked.

Mike playfully flexed his biceps. "Yeah. We're two of a kind," he joked back.

Nicole laughed. He really was an awfully sweet guy. Maybe he wasn't super smooth and romantic like Luc—but was that necessarily such a bad thing? With Mike, she almost never felt that weird off-kilter sense of heart-pounding uncertainty that Luc so often brought out in her without even seeming to try. Luc always kept her guessing, kept her on her toes. Being with Mike felt more like being

with an old friend, someone as comfortable as a favorite pair of jeans.

Okay, I'm really not looking for romance during this little Paris interlude, Nicole thought, gazing at Mike over the rim of her glass as she took a sip. *But if I were, Mike just might be a much more sensible choice than Luc.*

Chapter Eight

"We'd better hurry." Nicole checked her watch as Annike unlocked the apartment door. "We're supposed to meet those guys in just over an hour."

"Don't worry." Annike swung open the door. "It should only take us twenty minutes to get there. We have plenty of time."

It was a little before six o'clock, a couple of days after Nicole's dinner with Mike. She and Annike had just been released from a full day's filming. For once it hadn't rained at all, and they'd accomplished a lot. The directors had been so pleased that they'd given everyone the next day

off so they'd have a chance to edit the film. To celebrate, Mike had suggested they all get together that night for dinner, and most of the group had agreed.

Nicole followed Annike into the apartment. She was about to sling her bag onto the sofa when she heard her phone ring. When she pulled it out, she recognized Luc's number.

Her heart gave a nervous thump. She hadn't spoken to him since parting ways in front of that restaurant, though that was really no surprise—during their window shopping, Luc had mentioned that he would be working all the next day and evening.

"Hello?" she said.

"Bonsoir, chérie," he greeted her. "How is the most beautiful American citizen in Paris this evening?"

She smiled with relief. He sounded just the same as always. She hoped that meant he'd forgotten all about the awkward moment with Mike the other night.

"I'm fine," she said. "Just got home—they worked us hard today. We spent the whole morning doing testimonials at the Jardin du Luxembourg, then we had to rush all the way up to the Champs-Élysées for some holiday exterior shots with all the lights and decorations and everything."

"Sounds festive," Luc said. "Are you too exhausted to step out for a bit of dinner? *Tu es libre?* I know of a wonderful new place in the Latin Quarter…"

Nicole hesitated. "Sorry," she said. "*Je ne peux pas.* I can't do it tonight."

"C'est dommage."

He sounded so disappointed that she was tempted to invite him along with the group that night; she knew Annike and the others wouldn't mind. But she couldn't help thinking it just wasn't a good idea to bring Luc into the mix. For one thing, she didn't relish the thought of putting him and Mike together again after their last uncomfortable encounter. Nicole knew how competitive guys could get over every little thing.

And that was okay, she decided. She didn't have to accept every invitation that came her way.

"How about lunch tomorrow instead?" she asked. "I have the day off from filming if you're free then."

"*Cela me ferait un grand plaisir.* I have to work at the restaurant in the evening, but I am available until then. I shall call you in the morning to make plans."

"Great." Nicole said good-bye and hung up, feeling relieved. She wandered into the bedroom, where she found Annike sorting through her suitcases.

"What are you going to wear tonight?" Annike asked, glancing up. "Any chance I might borrow your blue sweater?"

"Sure. But only if I can wear your red one—it goes better with my black skirt."

The two girls spent the next half hour getting dressed,

primping, and goofing around. Nicole even took out her camera and snapped a few pictures.

Annike shrieked when Nicole took a photo of her flossing her teeth. Then she laughed. "Promise me you will not put these on the Internet if by chance I should end up doing that BBC program," she exclaimed. "It could be the end of my television career!"

Nicole smiled, but she also felt a jolt of guilt. In the busyness of the past few days, she'd all but forgotten about her friend's big decision. "Have you thought any more about what you want to do about that?" she asked.

Annike waved away the question. "Let's not speak about that right now, all right?" she begged with an apologetic smile. "Tonight is a night for fun! No serious decisions allowed."

"Fair enough," Nicole agreed with a laugh. "Now hurry up, I want to get a picture of you adjusting your underwear before it's time to leave . . ."

"Ah, here they are!" Mike cried as Nicole and Annike entered the crowded bistro and headed toward the large table in the back where the rest of the S.A.S.S. gang was sitting. "We were just about to send out a search party."

He stood and hurried to greet them. Nicole felt a bit uncomfortable as all eyes turned toward them. To hide her feelings, she pulled out her camera. "Smile, everyone," she said, snapping a few photos of the table.

"Oi, Nic, wait!" Quinn shouted with a loud hoot of laughter. "You caught my bad side!" She slung an arm around Yelena, who was sitting beside her, and struck an exaggerated pose. "There, that's better!"

Nicole took another picture, then stepped toward the table. Mike was still hovering nearby, a smile on his face.

"Come on," he said. "I saved you two some seats over here."

Seconds later Nicole was seated between Mike and Annike. There were at least a dozen people crammed around a table meant for no more than six or eight, so space was tight. Every time Mike reached for his glass or turned to speak to the person on his other side, his shoulder brushed against Nicole's.

Already feeling a little uncomfortable—how could being part of such a big group suddenly feel like a date?—she thought about going to the ladies' room and then taking a different seat when she returned. There was an empty one beside Melina, a sweet, cheerful girl from Greece who had been in her filming group that day. But she told herself she was being silly.

If Annike were waiting for me somewhere, she'd save me a seat by her, she thought. *Why should it be any different just because Mike is a guy?*

"I'm going to order a soda," she said to Annike. "Want one?"

Mike overheard and turned toward her. "Do you need

the waiter?" he asked. Without waiting for an answer, he half stood and waved his arm. *"Garçon!"* he called out. "Over here, *s'il vous plaît.*"

"Thanks," Nicole said. "But you really didn't have to do that."

"Oh, I don't mind." Mike beamed at her, leaning one arm on the back of her chair. "It was my pleasure."

Nicole bit her lip, wanting to say something in response but not quite sure what. That dinner the other night was initially intended to be as "just friends," but had Mike somehow read her mind about thinking he'd make a good boyfriend under different circumstances? She wasn't entirely sure where their friendship was headed. Had she led him on, made him think they were *already* more than friends? Nicole didn't think of them as anything like a couple, but did Mike?

She stewed over that off and on for the next hour or so as the group ordered food and gossiped about the S.A.S.S. filming. Even when Nicole tried to throw herself into the fun, she couldn't help remaining uncomfortably aware all the while of Mike sitting right beside her, hanging on her every word and laughing hysterically at her every lame joke.

Finally even Quinn noticed. As Mike chimed in on a discussion of language skills with an enthusiastic comment on how quickly Nicole had become proficient in

French, the British girl glanced at them curiously from across the table.

"Hang on," she said, her voice as usual more than loud enough to carry over the noise in the restaurant. "You two are looking rather cozy over there. Not about to start snogging right in front of us, are you?"

Mike chuckled. He didn't bother to move his arm, which was once again draped across the back of Nicole's chair. "Why? Hoping for a show?"

Quinn shouted with laughter and elbowed Yelena. "Hear that?" she said. "Guess that's a yes, eh? Well, let me be the first to say that you and Nic make a cute couple. Cheers!" She lifted her glass.

Nicole could feel her face turning red. "Ha-ha, very funny," she said, trying to hold back her annoyance. Quinn hadn't gotten any more tolerable since that encounter at the Musée d'Orsay, but Nicole had mostly managed to stay out of her way until tonight.

"So," Annike said loudly, obviously trying to change the subject. "What's everyone have planned for the day off tomorrow?"

Yelena cleared her throat. "Well, I am thinking—" she began in her soft, Russian-accented voice.

"I know what Nic and Mike have got planned," Quinn interrupted, still grinning across the table. "All-day snogging session!" She reached for Nicole's camera, which

she'd set on the table beside her plate. "Shall I take some snaps of the happy pair?"

"Quinn, you're too much!" Mike said with a laugh. "Did anyone ever tell you you've got a big mouth?"

"All the time, mate. All the time." Quinn grabbed the camera and aimed it. "But I just call it like I see it."

Nicole gritted her teeth, her blood boiling. Mike didn't seem bothered by Quinn's teasing. But Nicole was.

Taking a few deep breaths, she did her best to calm down and let it go. But she couldn't help flashing back to the last time she'd let Quinn's obnoxiousness slide. She was here to have a good time tonight, not to spend the rest of the evening stewing over some thoughtless girl's stupid jokes.

"Go on, Nic," Quinn urged. "If you're too bashful for some public snogging, at least let the poor boy have a feel under the table, or—"

"Give it a rest, Quinn!" Nicole's words came out even sharper than she'd intended them. "You're way off here. Mike and I are just friends, okay? There's absolutely nothing romantic between us. Got it? So just lay off already!"

Her voice cut through the noise like a knife. A hush fell over the entire table, and suddenly everyone seemed very busy with their own food.

Quinn looked taken aback. "Well, sor-r-ry!" she said, setting down Nicole's camera. "I was just having a bit of fun." She rolled her eyes and turned away. Annike turned and said something to Hamadi, who was sitting beside her, then Melina leaned across the table to respond, and with that, normal conversation resumed.

Nicole smiled, feeling proud of herself for standing up to the other girl this time. But that feeling fizzled as soon as she glanced over at Mike. He was looking back at her with a completely crestfallen expression on his face.

"Mike," she said quickly. "Um, listen. I'm sorry if that sounded harsh just now. I didn't mean—"

"It's all right," he said before she could finish. "You were right. Quinn was getting a little out of control. She shouldn't have said that stuff."

"Right." Nicole bit her lip, feeling terrible. The last thing she wanted to do was hurt Mike—whether or not she wanted to date him seriously, she already considered him a friend. "Still, I just meant—well, you know we're friends, right? We've said that all along."

"Of course." Mike shot her a smile, though it looked a bit forced. "No biggie."

But for the next half hour or so, he didn't quite seem to meet her eye. And when Hamadi announced that he was tired and heading home, Mike stood up immediately and offered to split a taxi with him.

"See you all after our day off," he added to the group at large, fishing in his pocket and pulling out a handful of euros, which he dropped in the middle of the table.

"Mike, wait…" Nicole began, feeling guilty.

He gave her a squeeze on the shoulder as he pushed past her chair. “Catch you later, Nicole.”

With that, he was gone. Nicole slumped in her seat, suddenly feeling like the wicked witch of Paris as she watched him wend his way through the crowded restaurant toward the door.

Chapter Nine

"Ça te plaît?" Luc asked, gesturing toward Nicole's plate.

"It's good," she replied, taking another bite of her salad. She glanced around the quiet bistro where they were having lunch. "This is a nice place."

He smiled. "Only the best for you, *chérie*."

"I bet you say that to all the girls," she joked, reaching for her water glass.

"Ah, you are too clever—you have caught me. Indeed I do." He winked. "But I mean it only with you."

Nicole laughed. Despite lingering feelings of guilt over

how Mike had left the night before, she was in a good mood. She'd slept late that morning, then she and Annike had gone to breakfast at a charming little café near the flat and then done some shopping until it was time for Nicole to meet Luc.

Aside from the Mike situation, the only thing that kept intruding and spoiling her mood a bit was her concern for Annike over her big decision. Annike was good at putting on a cheerful face, but Nicole knew her pretty well. With each passing day, she could sense that her friend was growing more anxious over her future. If only Nicole could help her more...

"*Qu'est-ce qu'il y a,* Nicole?" Luc leaned forward and peered at her. "Your eyes, they are miles away."

Nicole shook her head. "I was just thinking about Annike," she admitted. "She told you about her big TV opportunity, right?"

"Ah, yes." He nodded. "Her chance to be a star for all the world to see. An exciting opportunity indeed."

"Right. But I think she's really worried about what her family will think if she goes, and also whether she'd be shortchanging her future by interrupting her education like that. Then again, if she doesn't go, she may always wonder what she might have missed, you know? It's not an easy decision for her."

Luc shrugged and smiled. "*Ça s'arrangera.* She will

make the right decision, because whatever decision she makes will be right."

Nicole didn't find that philosophy particularly helpful, given that Annike had yet to make the decision in the first place. Then again, why should she be surprised? She already knew that Luc had a *c'est la vie* way of looking at life sometimes. He tended not to take things very seriously—flirting and kissing foremost among them. Why should something like a major, life-changing educational decision be any different? For a moment she thought back to that conversation in Printemps about his own future. Somehow, though, she suspected it was the wrong time to bring that up.

"Whatever," she said, deciding to trade in the serious subject for something a little more easy and fun. "Listen, I still have no idea what to get anyone for Christmas. Any brilliant new ideas?"

They spent the rest of the meal chatting about that. After they finished eating, Luc offered to take her shopping. "Perhaps we can find the perfect gifts for your friends today."

"That sounds great," Nicole agreed. "I'll be tied up in filming at the Louvre tomorrow, so I don't know when else I'll have time. Let's go."

They left the bistro and wandered along through the narrow, twisting streets of the Latin Quarter, stopping off

in any shops that caught their eye and browsing through the *bouquinistes'* stalls along the river. It was another cold, damp day, but there were still plenty of people out on the streets.

After a while the two of them followed the sound of lively holiday music and soon found themselves stepping into the Place Saint-Michel, a bustling square overlooked by an impressive nineteenth-century fountain. The Christmas carol was coming from an enthusiastic if slightly raggedy-looking band made up of what appeared to be students from the nearby Sorbonne. Nicole had never been in that particular square before, and she stared up at the enormous fountain curiously.

"What's going on there?" she asked, squinting at the male figure at the center of the fountain, who appeared to be wielding some sort of weapon over a prone shape at his feet.

"Why, that is Saint Michel, *bien entendu.* He is slaying a dragon," Luc replied. He stepped closer and looped one arm around her waist. "Perhaps he was doing it to impress a beautiful woman, eh?"

"Perhaps." Nicole sidled away, trying to extricate herself from his embrace. They were having such a relaxed, pleasant time today—she didn't want to spoil it.

But Luc wasn't so easily put off.

"Are you running away from me, *chérie*?" he teased.

Nicole rolled her eyes. But she also felt herself shiver—

and not from the cold weather—as Luc touched her cheek with his free hand.

"It is cold outside, *mon amie,*" he said. "Your skin, it is like ice. Perhaps we should find a way to warm you up?"

Nicole pushed him away. "No, thanks. I'm fine." She tried to keep her voice light, though she wasn't entirely successful. How many times was she going to have to fend off Luc's advances before he got the hint?

Clearly picking up on the tension in her voice, Luc immediately stepped back. "Then again, perhaps not." He checked his watch. "In any case, I am afraid I must go. I am expected at work soon."

"Okay." Nicole sighed, staring up at the Saint Michel fountain. Why did everything always have to be so difficult? She wished that just once during this visit to Paris she could spend some time with a guy and not have it end on a sour note.

Back at the flat, there was a note from Annike saying she'd gone out to lunch with her host family from the previous year. Nicole took advantage of the quiet moment to check her e-mail, hand wash a few things in the sink, and reorganize her luggage.

She was just sending off an e-mail to Patrice when there was a knock at the door. She swung it open and was surprised to see Mike standing there.

"Hi," he said with a rather sheepish smile. "Sorry for just

dropping by like this, but I was in the neighborhood. Are you busy?"

"Um, not really," Nicole said. "Want to come in?"

She stepped back and Mike entered and looked around. "Cute place," he said. "You and Annike are both staying here?"

"Is that a polite way of saying it's the tiniest apartment you've ever seen?" Nicole asked with a laugh.

Mike grinned. "Something like that," he said. "But you should see my place—it makes yours look like Notre Dame." He reached into his coat pocket and pulled out a small, gift-wrapped box. "But listen, you're probably wondering why I'm here. The thing is, I feel kind of bad for acting like such a big dork last night."

"Oh?" Nicole wasn't sure whether to acknowledge that she'd noticed his behavior or not.

He shrugged. "I'll admit it, Nicole. I've been attracted to you from the start. So when you said that last night—well, let's just say my male ego took a beating. But I deserved it. You've said all along that you're not interested in anything more than friendship right now, and I guess I haven't been listening well enough." He held out the box. "So this is my way of apologizing and saying I hope you still want to be friends. Merry Christmas."

Nicole was touched by his speech. It couldn't have been easy to admit to all that so frankly.

"Thanks," she said, accepting the gift. "But you didn't have to get me anything."

Mike shrugged. "It's no big deal. Just something that made me think of you—in a friends kind of way, I mean." He winked. "Open it."

Nicole ripped off the wrapping and opened the box. Inside was a small, colorful item. At first she couldn't tell what it was.

She picked it up for a better look and smiled. Now she recognized that brightly colored figure. It was a tiny plastic rendering of the Firebird, the largest animated figure from the Stravinsky Fountain near the Pompidou Center—one of her favorite spots in Paris. However, this version of the figure was wearing a tiny Santa hat. A silver tag attached to it read *Joyeux Noël.*

"It's a key chain." Mike was watching her face. "I know it's kind of dorky, but you mentioned you liked that fountain, so..."

"No, I love it!" Nicole said sincerely. "Thank you. And thank you for being so understanding about last night, too." She smiled at him with a sudden rush of affection. He really was an awfully nice guy. "You know, Mike, I'm really glad I met you. And when I tell you I'm not looking for a relationship right now, I hope you understand that that's all it is—it's not personal at all. In fact, if we'd met when we were both at home—Well, never mind." She realized she was babbling with relief at not having to feel like such a big meanie anymore. "Anyway, thanks for the key chain. It's great. I'm sorry I don't have anything for you."

Mike smiled and took a step toward her. "You're welcome," he said. "And you don't have to get me anything. I'd settle for a thank-you hug."

Nicole hesitated only momentarily before nodding and stepping forward. He engulfed her in a big bear hug, then pulled back slightly to look at her while still keeping his arms wrapped around her. He smelled faintly of aftershave and rain.

"And hey," he added softly, smiling down at her, "you might not realize this, but I'm a pretty patient guy. It won't be *that* long before we both *are* back home again. So we'll have to see what happens then, right?"

Nicole couldn't help being flattered as he loosened his grip and stepped back. She was also relieved that he hadn't tried to press his luck with that hug. Once again, her thoughts wandered to Luc, imagining what he might have done in the same situation. But she shook off such thoughts quickly.

"I'd better go." Mike glanced at his watch. "I'm supposed to meet Hamadi soon. But I'm glad I stopped by."

"Me, too," Nicole said.

"How about dinner sometime soon?" he asked. "Is that sort of thing still allowed for a couple of friends-for-now?"

"Sure," Nicole said. "I can't make any plans until I talk to Annike. But we can figure something out in a few days or whatever."

"Sounds good." Mike reached out and briefly squeezed her shoulder. "See you then."

As she shut the door behind him, Nicole realized she was smiling. It was true that Mike was no Monsieur Romance like Luc. But so what? Unlike Luc—or that adorable young tour guide she'd encountered in London, or the cute street performer in Dublin, or the variety of other foreign guys who'd flirted with her over the past few months—Mike wasn't a totally impractical love interest. As he'd just pointed out, they would both be going home to the same area after his semester and her travels were over. Maybe it would be worth giving him a chance when they were both back home in the U.S. of A.

She walked over to the window and looked out, staring at the ethereal metal spire of the Eiffel Tower in the distance. *Besides, spending time with Mike is just so... easy,* she thought. *There's no drama with him, no playing games or crazy heart-pounding sick-to-your-stomach doubt or obsessive wondering what he's* really *thinking or any of that kind of stuff. Hanging out with him is just sort of comfy and fun, almost like hanging with Annike or Patrice.*

And there's nothing wrong with that. Actually, a relationship like that might be kind of nice for a change...

Chapter Ten

Nicole shivered as a cold wind blew across the large, open courtyard outside the Louvre. "There they are," Annike said breathlessly, pointing. "By the pyramid."

The two girls hurried toward the group gathered near the large metal-and-glass pyramid that contained the entrance to the enormous classical museum. "Aha!" Nigel the director called as he spotted them. "Here are our stragglers now."

"Sorry we're late." Nicole rubbed her hands together for warmth. "There was a delay on the *métro*."

"Do not allow Nigel to make you feel any guilt," Adeline,

the native Parisian who had studied with S.A.S.S. in Finland, advised Nicole and Annike with a laugh. "He arrived only moments ago himself."

Nicole and Annike laughed along with the rest of the small group. Nigel pretended to be insulted but finally chuckled along.

"All right, then." He clapped his hands. "Let's get started. We're supposed to have everything we need on film by end of day tomorrow, and there's a lot to get through. So we're going to start off by trying to get some exterior work done here before it has a chance to start raining again." He shot a suspicious glance at the clouds scudding through the rather gray sky. "And they say *England* is wet..." he muttered before hurrying over to several camera operators who were standing nearby drinking coffee.

"*Bonjour*, everyone," Nicole said to the group at large. A quick glance around showed that today the group consisted of herself and Annike, Adeline and her friend Sylvie, Melina from Greece, the Egyptian newbie Hamadi, and a quiet, dignified Spanish girl named Isabel. "Did everyone enjoy the day off?"

"Oh, yes!" Melina exclaimed.

"Very much so," Hamadi added politely as Isabel nodded her head.

Sylvie smiled. "And now here we are, back to waiting for something to happen," she said. "Ah well, *qui va lentement va sûrement.*"

Nicole smiled back. At first she'd found Sylvie and Adeline a bit distant. But the whole group had grown friendlier the more time they'd all spent together. She was almost sorry they had only two more days together.

Just then Nigel returned. "All right, here's the plan," he said briskly. "I want you lot to spread out in two and threes all around this area here." He waved his arm to indicate the courtyard around the pyramid. "Just hang about and chat with one another, perhaps wander and pretend to be sight-seeing, that sort of thing. Should only take a moment to get some background shots that way, and then we'll move on. Just act naturally and pretend the cameras aren't here."

"Should we take bets on how long 'only a moment' will turn out to be?" Nicole joked as she and Annike obediently wandered off across the square. She had learned early on in this filming process not to expect anything to happen as quickly as Nigel claimed it would.

"Never mind," Annike said. "This will give us a chance to finish our chat about your new *amour*."

Nicole grimaced. She and Annike had spent most of the *métro* ride over discussing Mike's visit the day before.

"Let's not," she said. "I'm getting tired of going around and around about that—the more I try to make sense of what I should feel about him, the more confused I get. I mean, I really like Mike, and part of me thinks he and I could be really good together, you know? So why not give it a shot? But then I think I really shouldn't get mixed up in a relationship right now, and—Aargh! See what I mean?" She spread out her hands helplessly. "I'm totally repeating myself."

"It's all right." Annike smiled sympathetically. "We can talk about something else for a while."

"Like your big decision, maybe?" Nicole glanced over at her as they continued strolling around aimlessly.

Now it was Annike's turn to groan. "What is there to discuss about that?" she said. "The deadline is almost here, and I'm still no closer to deciding what I should do. I have been enjoying the filming, and it hasn't been a bother to be in the spotlight sometimes. But I still very much want to finish my education while I can, and I really enjoy my studies." She ran a hand through her straight blond hair. "I thought coming to Paris would help me to decide. Not only because of the filming, but just for some distance, you know?"

Nicole nodded. "It gives you a chance to get away from your everyday life and think."

"But that has not happened." Annike sounded frustrated. "In a way, I think I am finding it harder to reach a decision here. It is as if I have traveled back through time instead, when I did not have to worry about such things. Do you understand what I mean?"

"I think so." Nicole stopped walking and turned to face her. "I've been having a few S.A.S.S. flashbacks myself." She thought about Luc, and how easy it had been to fall right back into the old patterns with him.

Just then Sylvie and Adeline wandered by, chattering animatedly with each other in French, and Annike smiled as she watched them. “Still, in some ways it is so nice to be back, is it not?” she said. “It reminds me of all the fun we had. All the things we learned.”

“You mean like the art of French cooking?” Nicole teased. She and Annike had taken a cooking class together during their semester in Paris.

Annike laughed. “Something like that.” They both started walking again. “Seriously, though. I think if I had not done the S.A.S.S. program, I would not even be considering this London possibility.”

“I hear you.” Nicole thought about her life as it was now, compared to the life she'd had before Paris. “I know I learned a lot more than a little French and a little art history here last year. Mom and Dad are always saying that this place gave me a sense of independence and some better coping skills.” She felt a flash of premature nostalgia for Paris as she glanced around at the imposing façade of the Louvre surrounding them. “Sometimes I think I became a whole new person here.”

Annike reached over and squeezed her hand. “Me, too.”

“Okay, people.” Nigel sounded tired. It was almost four o'clock, and except for a brief lunch break, they'd been filming in the courtyard of the Louvre all day. The weather had held—in fact, it was warmer than it had been all week—and everyone had been afraid to stop. "Can you all stand one more reading of the last bit of today's script?"

"I'm not sure," Hamadi joked, which made everyone laugh. "Well, all right," he added with a grin. "I suppose *one* more..."

Nicole yawned and stretched. It had been a long day, with plenty of hurry-up-and-wait as usual.

"Come, let's go sit down while we wait our turn." Annike gestured toward the line of folding chairs the camera guys had set up nearby. "My feet are crying out for mercy."

They walked over and sat down as Nigel called Isabel forward to read from the script for that day. Nicole stretched out her legs and glanced around. The courtyard was dotted with groups of tourists and others drawn out by the nice weather. She spotted one familiar-looking figure coming toward them.

"Hey, is that Luc?" she asked, sitting up and squinting.

Annike looked. "It is," she said. "What is he doing here?"

"I don't know." Nicole waved at Luc, who waved back but continued strolling toward them at the same unhurried pace.

Finally he was there, smiling down at the two girls. *"Bonjour,"* he greeted them. "I remembered that you said you'd be filming here today, so I took a chance that you would still be here. Annike, might I have a quick word with Nicole *si tu le veux bien*?"

"Of course!" Annike got up and hurried off toward Hamadi, Adeline, and Melina, who were standing nearby watching the filming.

Left alone with Luc, Nicole sat up very straight, suddenly feeling as if she didn't know where to put her hands. It didn't help that Luc looked uncharacteristically serious as he lounged beside her.

"Um, what is it?" she asked. "Why were you looking for me? Is something wrong?"

"I hope not," he replied. His voice, like his eyes and the set of his mouth, was solemn and a bit uncertain. "I could not wait any longer to speak with you—I have been thinking all day at work today about how I acted yesterday. I should not have pushed you that way, and I am sorry."

Nicole let out the breath she hadn't even realized she was holding. "It's okay," she said. "*Oublions le passé.* It was no big deal."

"But it was. I think my behavior, it made it seem as if I only like to spend time with you if we are kissing and hugging." He winked. "Of course that is always fun, *chérie*. But I did not wish you to believe that is all I think about with you. Do you understand me?" He spread out his hands in a gesture of helplessness. "Sometimes my English, it seems to fail me..."

"No, no, I understand." Nicole smiled at him. "I totally get it. And thanks—really."

Suddenly she felt much lighter, the exhaustion of the

long day gone in a flash. Until this moment, she hadn't quite realized how much yesterday's uncomfortable parting from Luc was still bugging her. She was really glad he'd stopped by to clear the air.

Seeing Annike looking toward them curiously, she waved her over. "You can come back now," she called.

Annike rejoined them. "Everything okay over here?"

"Absolutely," Nicole assured her.

"Oui," Luc agreed. He leaned back in his chair, glancing over at the filming. "So what are we doing here?" he asked, looking and sounding much more like his usual self. "Something exciting and glamorous, no doubt?"

"A typical Parisian experience," Annike said with a twinkle in her eye. "We're sitting around discussing philosophy while waiting for something to happen."

"Aha! My favorite activity." Luc laughed. "What sort of philosophy are we discussing?"

"Mostly how much our semester here in Paris changed our lives," Nicole admitted.

"I see." Luc looked amused but also thoughtful. "*Il est vrai.* Of course I was not able to observe the lovely Annike very closely..." He bowed his head in Annike's direction. "However, I did have—how do you say it?—a front-row seat for the transformation of Mademoiselle Nicole."

Annike laughed as Nicole rolled her eyes. "Transformation?" Nicole said. "Let's not get carried away."

"Ah, but it is true!" Luc insisted. "I see this as a good

thing, *mon amie*. You were, of course, lovely and charming from the moment you arrived. But by the time you said *au revoir* to Paris, you were much more than that. I am in awe of how you are now able to throw yourself into new experiences, learning as you go, rather than remaining with what is known and familiar and easy. *Tu comprends*?"

Nicole blinked. For some reason, what Luc was saying made her think of the way she'd been avoiding romantic involvement with Mike.

Am I doing it again? she wondered. *Falling into the old patterns, sticking with what's safe and easy? Back then it was being with Nate and having my life planned out, and now it's sort of the opposite, but is that just a new kind of cop-out? Keeping things casual with Luc is one thing...* She sneaked a quick peek at him. *But the situation with Mike is totally different. Like he said, we'll be going home to the same place eventually. I mean, sure, if I give things a shot with him right now, things might get complicated—after all, we'll both be traveling for the next four or five months, and who knows what could happen in that time. Then again, a lot about the two of us just seems to make sense somehow. Maybe I should just throw myself into it, as Luc just put it, and see what happens...*

Annike had nodded all through Luc's comments. "That's exactly it," she said. "At first, Nicole, you were a little bit hesitant to try new things. Remember? I had to nearly drag you along to taste a bit of *crêpe*."

Nicole knew her friend was being polite. She hadn't just been hesitant—she'd been downright resistant to all that Paris had to offer.

"I remember," she said. "I'm glad I'm not like that anymore. At least I try not to be."

Luc tilted his chair back, balancing on two legs as he gazed at her. *"Justement,"* he said. "And now I think you know what you want from life, Nicole. And you are not so affected by what other people want for you."

Annike sighed. "That is the lesson I need to study more," she admitted. "I still cannot decide whether I am being too affected by others' opinions on this television thing..."

After that, they discussed Annike's decision until it was time for her to take her turn in front of the cameras. "I hope she figures things out soon," Nicole fretted as Annike hurried off, feeling anxious on her friend's behalf. "She's so worried about this, and I know she has to reach a decision about it soon. I mean, Christmas Eve is tomorrow, and then she only has two more days until the deadline."

"That reminds me," Luc said. "I hoped we might get together on Christmas Day. My mother is traveling out to Guyancourt that morning to see her sister, and I have no other family in Paris. *Tu es libre?"*

"Sure, I think so." Nicole shrugged. "I was just planning to hang out with Annike anyway. Want to come over? Our place is small, but..."

"No, that is a perfect plan," Luc said with a smile. "I'd

love to join you. I shall be counting the hours until then."

Nicole bit her lip. "Me, too," she said. "And the way I'm counting, I *really* don't have much time left to finish my Christmas shopping."

"Ah, that is right." Luc shook his head. "I feel responsible—I am afraid I distracted you yesterday rather than helping you shop as I had promised. May I make up for this mistake by taking you out shopping again today?"

Nicole hesitated only briefly before nodding. After all, she *did* need to get her shopping done. And who better to help her than someone who knew the city as well as Luc did? Besides, she knew Luc was far too polite not to invite Annike along as well. She could be Nicole's buffer—the guarantee that things would stay on a strictly friendship level this time.

"Merci," she said. "That sounds great."

As it turned out, though, Annike had already made plans to have coffee with the others from their group. "Go on and have fun though, you two," she said. "But we're still on for dinner, Nicole, yes?"

"Definitely," Nicole said, ignoring the tiny shiver that ran through her body at the thought of more alone time with Luc. Even after his earlier apology, she knew there was no way of predicting what might happen. "I'll meet you back at the flat at six."

Despite all of her reservations, she and Luc almost

immediately fell into a comfortable, easy rapport. They shopped, chatted, and wandered the holiday-bedecked streets for more than an hour. At one point they stopped to peer in the lavishly decorated windows of a small bakery.

"What's that?" Nicole asked, pointing to a round cake with a gold paper crown perched on top of it.

Luc glanced that way. "Ah, but that is, of course, *a galette des rois*—the Three Kings' cake," he said. "Surely you have heard of it, *non*?"

"Oh, right, I think so." Nicole searched her mind, trying to remember what she'd heard about that particular French holiday tradition. "Um, isn't there something weird hidden inside it, like a marble or a breath mint or something? And whoever chokes on it becomes, like, president of France for an hour?" She blinked at him innocently, feigning great earnestness.

Luc stared at her for a second, then started laughing so hard he had to lean against the wall nearby. "Something like that, *oui*," he gasped out at last. "The item hidden inside is normally a small bean. Whoever finds it is named king or queen for the day."

"Hey, I was close." Nicole grinned and shrugged, feeling kind of proud of herself. Luc had a great sense of humor, but it normally tended toward the wry or ironic. She wasn't sure she'd ever seen him crack up like that.

They moved on, still talking and laughing and goofing

around. Nicole was a little sorry when she checked her watch and saw that it was past five thirty already.

"I'd better take off," she said. "I don't want to keep Annike waiting."

She tucked her camera away in her shoulder bag. She and Luc were in front of the famous Parisian department store Galeries Lafayette, where they'd just been posing and taking silly pictures of each other in front of the holiday displays.

"Mais bien sûr," Luc said. "Please allow me to walk you to the *métro*."

"Sure." Nicole was feeling good about life in general. Not only was she feeling positive about her friendship with Luc, but he'd actually helped her solve her gift-giving dilemma.

"This way. I know a shortcut." Luc led her around the next corner.

Nicole followed him down a narrow side street. But she stopped short as a brilliant string of silvery Christmas lights suddenly blinked on over the doorway of the small café they were passing, instantly transforming an ordinary doorway into a tableau worthy of the fanciest of the department stores out on the broad Parisian avenues.

"Ooh, it's beautiful!" Nicole stopped short, gazing up at the display.

Luc stepped over and looped an arm around her shoulders, looking up as well. *"Mais oui,"* he said. "And look—another lovely view."

Nicole looked where he was pointing and realized that the Eiffel Tower had just come into view over the tops of the buildings. Gazing up at it, she experienced a weird moment of déjà vu. Then she realized she was recalling another time when she and Luc had suddenly come upon a spectacular view of La Tour Eiffel. That time had ended in an unexpected but incredible kiss...

She shivered and looked up at him, only to find his green eyes already gazing down at her. They locked eyes for a moment, neither of them moving a muscle even as cars and trucks rumbled past on the narrow street and pedestrians buried in their winter wear hurried past all around them.

"Ah, Nicole," Luc said, though it came out as more of a sigh. *"Ma chérie..."*

Without further ado, he turned her toward him and kissed her. Nicole's heart was pounding furiously. She knew she should push him away—wasn't this undoing all the good of their little chat earlier? But somehow, she couldn't seem to do it. She couldn't seem to *want* to do it.

She kissed him back, grabbing onto the lapels of his coat and standing on tiptoes. Her eyes drifted shut, though even through the lids she could still see the bright holiday lights blinking on and off overhead. Her blood was rushing through her veins, and for a second she forgot all about anything and everything else except the passionate lips exploring hers.

He pulled back slightly. *"Ma chèrie,"* he murmured, his lips almost brushing hers as he spoke, his warm breath mixing with hers.

With that, she finally returned to her senses. "No, stop," she said with lips that were still tingling from that amazing kiss. She forced herself to push away from him. "We shouldn't do this. I have to go—I'm late."

"Je ne fais qu'entrer et sortir," Luc said, brushing a stray strand of hair off her face. "Annike will forgive you."

Nicole shuddered, tempted just to give in, as every cell in her body was urging her to do. But she did her best to resist that temptation.

"Sorry," she said breathlessly. "I really have to go!"

She raced off toward the *métro* station, not daring to look back. Because if she did, she was pretty sure she would be *really* late for that dinner with Annike...

By the time she arrived at the flat a short while later, she was still feeling a bit giddy and befuddled. Maybe she'd been overthinking things all along. Wasn't Luc the one who'd taught her that a kiss had to mean only as much as the two people involved wanted it to mean? She'd never quite been able to believe that, but maybe...

"Oh, there you are," Annike greeted her as she walked in. "Before I forget, I am supposed to ask you to call Mike."

"What?" Nicole was startled. With some difficulty, her mind lurched from Luc to Mike. "What do you mean? You talked to Mike?"

Annike nodded. "I ran into him when I had coffee with Yelena, Hamadi, and the others."

"Oh. Um, what did he want?"

"Didn't say. Just wanted you to call him."

"Okay." Nicole couldn't help feeling oddly guilty. She realized that she'd just about talked herself into making a go of things with Mike earlier. So if that was the case, how could she forget all about him and kiss Luc—especially like *that*? French kiss, indeed...

She felt even worse when she returned the call and Mike sounded incredibly glad to hear from her, as usual. "Remember how we were talking about grabbing some dinner sometime?" he said. "Well, I was just thinking—my folks are flying in from Geneva for Christmas Day, but I'm all alone tomorrow night for Christmas Eve. Want to keep each other company?"

Nicole hadn't discussed the next day's plans with Annike yet, but she figured her friend would understand whatever she decided. She was still feeling guilty about how she'd treated Mike during the incident with Quinn, and the kiss with Luc certainly hadn't helped.

"Sure," she blurted out before she could overthink it. "That sounds perfect."

Chapter Eleven

"...so I don't know if I should have said yes to having dinner with Mike tonight," Nicole mused aloud to Annike, squinting against the sun—which had emerged for once—to see if Nigel was ready to resume filming yet. "I mean, sure, I'd pretty much decided to give things a shot with him. But a date on Christmas Eve? That seems like a lot of pressure." She shrugged. "Then again, I guess it's only a big deal if I make it one. And if things do work out, I guess it will make a great how-we-got-together story, right?"

"Oui," Annike replied.

"By the way, it still feels totally weird that today is

Christmas Eve, doesn't it? It doesn't seem quite real."

"Yes," Annike said. "It is strange not to be at home."

Nicole glanced over at Nigel again. It was the final day of filming, and the entire group of fifteen or so student volunteers was gathered in the sculpture garden of the Musée Rodin. Nigel was talking with the crew while most of the students were gathered around the base of the famous statue *The Thinker*. Nicole had followed Annike, who had wandered off to look at the stark skeletons of some winter-dormant rosebushes nearby.

Mike was over with the rest of the students, staring up at the statue on its pedestal and chatting with Isabel and Hamadi. Nicole watched him, taking in the easy way he smiled and laughed. She also couldn't help noticing how nice he looked in his well-fitted jacket and butt-hugging jeans, his sandy hair tousled by the breeze. Most of the girls she'd known back in high school would totally drool over a guy like him...

She was distracted at that moment by a loud shriek of laughter, which seemed out of place in the frostbitten but still dignified sculpture garden. She frowned as she spotted Quinn dragging Yelena along with her in the opposite direction.

"Oi, Mikey!" Quinn shouted, waving a small digital camera in the air so vigorously that she almost bonked Melina in the head with it. "Come here a sec and take our piccy!"

"What's wrong with that girl?" Nicole muttered, watching as Quinn shoved her camera into Mike's hand and then rushed over to pose at the base of *The Thinker* with Yelena beside her. With a good-natured smile, Mike began snapping photos. "It's really pretty annoying how she's always bossing everyone around. Especially poor Yelena."

Her tone came out sounding more bitter than she'd planned. She shot a quick glance over at Annike, expecting her to smile and point out—quite rightly—that Nicole's own past history might be coloring her view of the other girls' friendship a bit.

But Annike was staring down at one of the dormant rose plants, not seeming to be paying attention. Nicole's stomach lurched as she realized she'd been babbling on about her own problems without noticing that Annike wasn't at all involved in the conversation.

"Hey," she said, stepping over and giving Annike a gentle poke in the shoulder. "You okay?"

"Hmm?" Annike blinked and looked up. "Oh, sorry. What were you saying?"

"Never mind. What are *you* thinking about? You're a million miles away."

Annike laughed and brushed back her hair. "Not quite that far," she admitted. "Just, um, fifteen hundred kilometers or so. You see, my mother called from Stockholm this morning."

"Oh, right." Nicole vaguely recalled hearing Annike's

phone ring as she'd stepped into the shower. "Wait—you didn't tell her, did you?"

"No." Annike sighed. "And I feel terribly guilty about it. I cannot go on much longer keeping this from them. But I really do wish to figure out what to do first. And my deadline is in two days. It is driving me crazy!"

Nicole felt like kicking herself—she should have noticed that Annike was troubled this morning. But she'd been too busy obsessing over her date with Mike and that kiss with Luc to notice a thing.

She opened her mouth to respond, but just then there was an even louder shout of laughter. Glancing over, she saw that Nigel was standing near *The Thinker* watching as Quinn and Yelena imitated the pose of the famous sculpture. Nicole couldn't help smiling a little despite her distaste for Quinn.

"Over here, people!" Nigel shouted. "Quinn's given us an idea..."

Soon the entire group was taking turns posing at the base of the statue. Nicole grinned as she watched Claude and Louis ham it up, scratching their chins and making funny faces.

"This was actually a cute idea," she said. "I bet it will be funny if they use it in the video."

"Hmm." Annike didn't look so sure.

"Nicole!" Nigel gestured for her to come forward. "You're up. Let's get the thinking cap on, shall we?"

Nicole giggled and hurried over. She did her best to imitate the pose and attitude of Rodin's masterpiece.

Next it was Annike's turn. "Oh, that's all right," she said. "I think I'll skip this one."

Nicole wasn't terribly surprised. Annike definitely knew how to have fun, but she also had a natural dignity that seemed a bit at odds with such a silly public pose.

"Aw, g'won!" Quinn called out. "Don't be a spoilsport!"

"Just have a go, Annike," Nigel added, checking his watch. "Then let's have everyone join her for a big group shot of the same."

Annike bit her lip, then nodded and stepped forward. Once she'd taken her turn, all the students crowded in and did the pose together while the camera guys filmed. At the end, Mike even pulled in a laughing Nigel to join them.

When they were finished, Nicole led Annike off a short distance to a fairly private spot behind a large yew. "Hey," she said. "If you really didn't want to do that pose, why'd you cave in?"

Annike shrugged. "It was not that important either way."

"Still, you didn't have to do it just because Nigel and the others wanted you to, you know."

"I know." Annike's expression held an uncharacteristic hint of annoyance as she met Nicole's gaze. "What is the big deal about this?"

Nicole stared back at her. She didn't want to make

Annike angry. But this seemed important, considering everything that was going on.

"I just hate seeing you worrying so much about doing what everyone else wants that you forget about what *you* want," she said. "That's all."

Annike looked taken aback for a moment. Then she sighed.

"You are right." She rubbed her chin. "That is just me, I'm afraid. I always want to please everyone and I feel guilty if I cannot." She waved a hand at *The Thinker.* "Sometimes it is small things, like this. But other times..."

"Are you thinking about your big decision again?" Nicole guessed.

"Yes. I suppose I've been too worried about pleasing everyone—my parents, Berg, the television people. It has been keeping me from admitting what it is that I really want." She shook her head. "In any case, thank you, Nicole."

"For what?"

Annike smiled. "For helping me reach a decision about the television issue."

"I did that?"

"Yes. Actually, I think I already knew what my answer has to be. But until you said what you did, I was hesitant to commit to my decision. It's just that I have very much enjoyed most of the S.A.S.S. filming and—"

"So does this mean you're going to do it? You're moving to London?" Nicole held her breath, already imagining it.

"*Nej.* I have decided I will not try out for the program. I wish to finish my education first. I am very happy with my life at university. It is all too much to give up, even for a short time." She reached out and squeezed Nicole's hands in hers. "And it is not only because that is what my parents would wish me to do. It is not about Berg, either. It is only for myself. As you say, that is what I must think of at this time."

Nicole couldn't help a quick flash of disappointment. It would have been fun to say she was friends with an international TV star. But that wasn't important—what was important was for Annike to do what she felt was right for her.

"So you are certain about this?" she asked with an encouraging smile.

Annike sighed. "Certain? That is, perhaps, too strong a word." She smiled ruefully. "Why is it so hard to know the best thing to do? It does seem rather unfair having to give up something so wonderful due only to bad timing."

"I know what you mean." Nicole couldn't help flashing to Luc. But she pushed that aside and reached out to give Annike a hug. "Anyway, congrats—I'm glad you decided. Now you can relax and enjoy the rest of this visit!"

"True." Annike laughed as she hugged her back, already sounding more like her lighthearted self. "You do know how to look on the bright side of things, Nicole."

"What can I say?" Nicole pulled back and smiled fondly at her friend. "I learned from the best."

"What are you going to wear out with Mike tonight?" Annike asked as they walked toward their building from the *métro* station.

"I'm not sure." Nicole's steps quickened. After wrapping up the filming, Nigel and the other directors had thanked them by taking everyone to a nearby café for coffee and Christmas pastries. Now it was getting late—Mike was due to pick her up soon. "By the way, are you sure you don't want to come with us? Mike won't mind."

Annike laughed. "I'm not so sure about that!" she teased as they hurried into their building and headed up the stairs. "In any case, I shall be fine. I told you, I am going to my host family's house for a while, then meeting up with some of the gang from filming later."

Whatever Nicole might have said next was forgotten as she reached the top of the stairs and saw Luc standing in the hallway, looking ridiculously adorable in dark slacks and a burgundy Irish-knit sweater. Her heart fluttered and she stopped short, flooded with the intense memory of the last time she'd seen him.

"*Joyeux Noël,* Nicole," he said. "And to you as well, Mademoiselle Annike," he added as Annike reached the hall behind Nicole.

"Luc! What are you doing here?" Annike asked. She shot Nicole a quick, curious glance. Nicole had told her all about that kiss the day before, of course. Now Nicole could almost see the thought balloon forming over her friend's head.

Luc reached into his coat pocket. "Ah, but it is a secret," he told Annike playfully. "Nicole would not wish you to know."

For one crazy moment Nicole thought he was talking about their kiss. Then he pulled a small paper bag out of his pocket and she realized the truth. She'd noticed after arriving home the night before that she'd forgotten that particular small shopping bag, which he'd tucked into his pocket to carry for her while they were walking around.

No wonder, she thought, mentally wandering back again to that incredible, confusing kiss. *My mind wasn't exactly on shopping at that point...*

Luc stepped toward her. "So," he said with a smile. "What do you lovely ladies have planned this evening?"

"Excuse me," Annike said with a grin, stepping around him to get to the apartment door. "Speaking of plans, I'm going to be late if I don't hurry."

"All right." Luc waved as Annike let herself into the flat, then returned his gaze to Nicole and winked. "Alone at last, *chérie.*"

Nicole gulped, hardly taking in his flirtatious words as she glanced at her watch and realized she was running even later than Annike. "Thank you for returning this," she said, taking the package from Luc's hand and walking him toward the stairs. "But I don't want to keep you—it's Christmas Eve, you know."

"I know." He gazed at her with amusement. "But do not worry; my mother, she will understand if I am a little late. Especially when I tell her I was delayed by a beautiful woman."

"I'm sure she will." Nicole took him by the arm, steering him more firmly toward the stairwell. She definitely didn't want him to be there when Mike arrived to pick her up. "She must be totally used to hearing those kinds of excuses from you by now."

Just then came the sound of heavy footsteps hurrying up the stairs. A moment later Mike's cheerful face appeared. He was dressed up and looking dapper in a tie and sport jacket.

As the two guys spotted each other, Nicole wished she could drop through the floor. Why oh why did Luc always have to witness her dates with Mike?

The last one wasn't really a date, she reminded herself during the endless moment of awkward silence, thinking back to that equally awkward accidental meeting in front of the Indian restaurant. Then she shook her head, realizing that such distinctions were pointless. *But for all Luc knows, Mike and I could have been dating hot and heavy all week. And then yesterday I totally make out with* him *instead... How do I get myself into these ridiculous situations, anyway? And more importantly, how am I supposed to get out of this one?*

Before she could figure it out, Mike stepped forward and stuck out his hand. "Merry Christmas, Luc," he said, so sincerely that Nicole had to wonder if some of his parents' diplomatic training hadn't rubbed off on him.

"Merci." Luc shook Mike's hand, only the rather tense set of his jaw revealing that anything might be wrong. "And the same to you. *Bonsoir*." Widening his glance to include Nicole, he turned and hurried off down the stairs.

"Bye," Nicole said, though by then he was already gone.

That evening Nicole had a mostly pleasant time out with Mike. The holiday gave Paris an extra romantic feeling, and as the two of them enjoyed an unhurried meal at a nice restaurant followed by a performance of *The Nutcracker* at a local theater, it was easy to drift automatically into a boyfriend/girlfriend sort of mood.

And of course Mike did nothing to discourage that. He was a perfect gentleman—pulling out her chair, pouring her wine, guiding her whenever they walked anywhere with a hand on the small of her back. Neither of them had mentioned the encounter with Luc, though it kept popping into Nicole's head at odd times.

As she watched the dancers twirl onstage in the last act of the ballet, Nicole was starting to have a strange, out-of-body feeling, almost as if she were floating up at the top of the theater somewhere looking down at herself. There she was, a pretty American girl sitting beside a handsome American guy. They made the perfect couple in just about every way. They looked good together. They got along well. They had a lot in common.

So then why did she feel so weird about being here?

It's probably just because it's Christmas Eve, she thought. *I've never been away from my family on Christmas. Of course it's going to seem kind of strange.*

That was part of it, certainly. But was it the whole answer? She couldn't help thinking back to Luc's expression when Mike had turned up earlier. The first time that had happened, Luc had looked startled, yes, and annoyed, and perhaps a bit jealous. But this time had been different somehow. Was it her imagination, or had she also seen hurt in his eyes when he'd realized why Mike was there?

"This is good, isn't it?" Mike whispered, breaking into her thoughts as he leaned closer. "I can't believe I'm sitting here seeing the ballet in Paris. My buddies back home wouldn't believe it!"

Nicole forced a smile. But she was glad the music gave her an excuse not to answer. Because all of a sudden she couldn't quite shake the idea that the reason she might be feeling so weird about being here was that she just might be here with the wrong guy.

• • •

"This was fun." Mike smiled down at Nicole, his hands in the pocket of his coat. They were standing in front of her building. It was late, and the cold, lamplit streets were deserted and quiet apart from the occasional car driving past and, from an upper window of the building next door, the muffled sound of a piano playing a melancholy French carol.

"It *was* fun," Nicole said. "Thanks."

Mike stepped forward. Taking one hand out of his pocket, he rested it on her shoulder, then bent down and kissed her softly on the lips.

"You're welcome," he said. "It was my pleasure. I hope we can do it again soon. In fact, what are you doing tomorrow?"

"Tomorrow?"

"Like I told you, my folks are flying in tomorrow morning to spend Christmas Day here before heading home. I'd love for you to meet them—do you want to stop by for brunch or something?"

Nicole felt frozen in place, not sure what to say. It would be easy just to nod and agree, to go and meet Mike's parents tomorrow and see what happened from there. But suddenly she knew that would be all wrong. She could still feel the imprint of Mike's lips on hers, but that was all it felt like—a pair of lips pressing against her own. It was nothing at all like what she'd felt when she and Luc had kissed.

This is no time to be wishy-washy, she told herself. *Wasn't I just getting on Annike's case about that sort of thing?*

She still had no idea what to think or feel about Luc, no matter how tingly she felt when she remembered that kiss, or how much her heart jumped and fluttered whenever he was around. But no matter what happened with Luc, tonight had helped her realize one thing. Her heart was never going to flutter that way for Mike. He was a great guy who was perfect for her, at least on paper. But her heart hadn't gotten the memo. Not even after this evening—Christmas Eve in Paris, for Pete's sake! It had been an incredible date that should have been amazingly romantic, but that single kiss had made it perfectly clear that she was never going to see Mike as anything more than a friend.

"I'm sorry," she said. "I don't think so."

"Oh." Mike's face fell, then he shrugged. "Okay. You don't leave town for another week, though, right? So maybe we could—"

"Wait." She stopped him with a hand on his arm. "I—I don't think this is going to work. I really like you, but, um, not in that way. I think we should stay just friends."

He frowned slightly. "This isn't about the traveling thing again, is it?" he said. "Because like we talked about, it'll only be a few months before we're both in the same place."

"That's not the problem." Nicole did her best to keep

her voice kind yet firm. She didn't want to leave any room for misinterpretation—that wouldn't be fair to him. "I'm really, really sorry to do this to you on Christmas Eve, Mike, but I'm just not feeling a spark between us, and I like you way too much to let things go on this way any longer. I'm sorry."

Mike's shoulders slumped. "Okay, I hear you." He sighed. "I guess maybe I should've seen this coming after finding you with that Luc guy again today, huh?"

"This isn't about Luc," Nicole said quickly. "This is only about you and me. And I hope we can still be friends." She shrugged and smiled slightly. "I know that sounds like a corny line, but I mean it. You're a cool guy, Mike. I'm glad I met you."

"Me, too." He smiled wanly. "Merry Christmas, Nicole."

"Merry Christmas."

As she climbed the stairs to the flat, Nicole found she still couldn't stop thinking about those two very different kisses. Looked at with an objective eye, they hadn't started out very differently at all. Both had been initiated at an opportune moment by guys who were clearly attracted to her. However, her responses had been as different as night and day. That had to mean something.

Still, Luc lived in Paris, and she lived in the United States. She would only be in town for a few more days, and Luc already seemed so distracted by his jobs and school.

And she still had several months of traveling to do. Was it really fair to either of them to risk the nice friendship they had going now—when they had no realistic romantic future together beyond next week?

Chapter Twelve

From: PatriceQT@email.com

To: NicLar@email.com

Subject: Merry Merry!

Hey Nic,

I miss u! Xmas isn't the same w/o u here! But I hope ur having fun in Paris! I got ur e-mail last night; too bad things didn't work out w/u and Mike. Whatever happened w/Luc? U haven't mentioned him lately. I want 2 hear the scoop!

But 4 now, Merry Christmas! I'm off 2 open presents

now—whee! Write back when u have a chance & tell me all about Xmas in Paris!

Love & kisses,

Patrice

From: Larsons9701@email.com

To: NicLar@email.com

Subject: Merry Christmas, Nicole!

Hi sweetie,

Just writing to say Merry Christmas. Dad and I are missing you like crazy. Although it hardly feels like Christmas at all here in the great dry Southwest. Christmas is supposed to be cold, ha-ha!

We'll call you tonight. But have a nice French Christmas in the meantime. We can't wait to see you and celebrate properly next month. (Dad is already polishing up his college German in preparation, ha-ha!)

Jingle jingle!

Love,

Mom (and Dad)

"Is that someone at the door?" Annike looked up from setting out cookies on a paper plate in the tiny apartment kitchen.

"I'll get it."

Nicole hurried toward the door. It was Christmas Day, and the two of them were getting ready to host what they were jokingly calling their "Nobody Loves Us in Paris" Christmas get-together for all those who had no family or other friends in the area. Annike had invited several more people the night before, and she and Nicole had spent all morning tidying up the flat and preparing some Christmas treats. Nicole was glad that Annike had thought to do some shopping for food and drinks on the same afternoon she'd been so distracted by her gift-shopping expedition with Luc. Otherwise they would have had nothing to serve their guests but crackers and Orangina!

She hadn't spoken to Luc since their encounter in the hallway the evening before. Even after her big decision about Mike, she still had no idea what to do with her feelings for Luc. And now, at the thought that he would soon be arriving, her stomach was in knots. As she reached for the doorknob she took a deep breath, doing her best to prepare herself to face him.

But when she swung open the door, it wasn't Luc standing there, but Yelena. The Russian girl was dressed in a pretty blue dress and carrying a paper grocery bag.

"*Joyeux Noël,* Nicole," she said in her soft, shy voice. "And *Pozdrevlyayu s prazdnikom Rozhdestva is Novym Godom.* That is how we say it in Russia."

"Merry Christmas." Nicole smiled at her. "Come on in—you're the first one to arrive."

Annike looked up as Yelena entered. "You made it!" she cried with obvious delight. "*God Jul*—I'm so glad you decided to join us after all!"

"I almost did not," Yelena admitted. "Quinn very much wanted me to come with her. She is visiting friends of her family out in Argenteuil for today." She set down her bag of food on the counter and unbuttoned her coat. "But I say to her, I rather feel more comfortable with friends from S.A.S.S. than people I do not know."

Nicole could tell the Russian girl was a little worried about her decision. "You definitely made the right choice," she assured her. "We're going to be way more fun than a bunch of strangers out in the burbs."

"Burbs?" both Annike and Yelena repeated in confusion.

Nicole laughed. She was still explaining herself when someone else knocked on the door. This time it was Melina, the girl from Greece.

"*Kala Christouyenna*, everyone!" she cried out joyfully. "I hope I am not too early! But if I am, you must forgive me, for I bring a lot of food! I have even some *christopsomo*—that is Christmas bread from Greece, I find it right here in Paris!"

Melina was soon followed by a guy from New Zealand

named Brendan who had been in Nicole's filming group a couple of times, along with Isabel and finally Hamadi. Each of them had also brought some bit of food or drink to add to the holiday feast, and Melina had also brought her iPod and some minispeakers. Soon the counter and coffee table were filled with appetizing treats and the apartment with the sounds of music—Christmas and otherwise—along with talking and laughter.

Nicole had just checked her watch for the third time when there was another knock on the door. This time when she opened the door she found Luc smiling at her from the hallway. He looked as relaxed and handsome as ever in jeans and a black jacket; a bottle was tucked under one arm.

"Joyeux Noël, chérie," he said, immediately stepping forward and planting a kiss on each of Nicole's cheeks. "Thank you for inviting me."

"*Joyeux Noël.* Come on in." Nicole had the uncomfortable feeling that she was blushing. But she did her best to seem normal as she introduced Luc to the people he didn't know in the group. Whatever deep thoughts she'd been having about him, this wasn't the time to worry about their relationship. It was Christmas—that was enough for right now.

She had been a bit concerned about how Luc would fit into the group, but she needn't have worried. Even Yelena was soon laughing at his comments and jokes.

"Ah, but Luc," Annike exclaimed at one point as she carried another pitcher of coffee out from the kitchen. "We were hoping you might arrive dressed as Père Noël for this occasion."

Luc chuckled. He was lounging on the sofa between Hamadi and Melina, his long legs sprawled out beneath the coffee table. "I am sorry to disappoint you, Annike, *mon amie.* In any case, for such an international gathering as this, I would not know whether to come dressed as Papa Noël, or perhaps the American Santa Claus or Tomte the Swedish Christmas gnome." He reached for a cookie from the platter in front of him and then glanced at Yelena, who was sitting on the floor nearby giggling at the whole exchange. "Mademoiselle Yelena, *je me demande*—do you have such things as Christmas trees and Santa Claus in Russia?"

"The trees we do have, yes," Yelena replied, sitting up a little straighter and tucking her feet beneath her. "But not exactly the Santa Claus. However we do have Saint Nicholas and also Babouschka, a grandmother woman who brings gifts to children. Oh, and also we do not normally, um…" She said a word in Russian and glanced at Annike for help.

Annike pursed her lips. "Sorry, not certain about that one," she said. "Um, perhaps you mean celebrate?"

"Yes, *merci,* that is it exactly!" Yelena's face lit up. Nicole couldn't help observing that she really was pretty when

she smiled. "We all do not celebrate Noel on twenty-fifth of December, but on sixth of January. That is because Russian Orthodox Church has different calendar for holy days." She smiled and shrugged. "And the older people, they are always reminding us that under communism, it was not allowed to have Noël at all. Instead they must used New Year's Day for giving of gifts, and with no Saint Nicholas allowed, they changed to Grandfather Frost."

"Wow." Nicole was leaning on the back of the chair where Isabel was sitting. Her travels so far had been showing her that in a lot of ways people were really very similar the world over. But listening to Yelena and realizing that it hadn't really been that long since Yelena's country had been part of the Soviet Union—something that had seemed so long ago and foreign and far away when she'd learned about it in history class—reminded her that there were still some real differences, too.

"Grandfather Frost—I like that!" Melina said with interest. "In Greece, our Saint Nicholas is the patron saint of sailors and so he is often pictured for us with seawater dripping from his beard. Also, we do not have as many Christmas trees as they do here in France. Instead nearly every home will have a wooden bowl with a bit of basil and a small cross." She smiled, which brought out dimples in her full, olive-skinned cheeks. "And do not get me started on the *killantzaroi*—those are naughty goblins who appear at Christmastime to cause trouble. We keep them away with the basil water and also by keeping a fire burning at all times."

"What about you, Isabel?" Annike had set down the coffee by now and was perched on the arm of the sofa. "What is Christmas like in Spain?"

"Well, I suppose it is much like here in France," Isabel responded. "Nothing so interesting as naughty goblins, certainly!"

Everyone laughed at that, especially Melina. "It's the same with us Kiwis," Brendan put in. "The most interesting thing we do that's a bit different is that we generally have a barbecue for Christmas. But I s'pose that's because it falls in the summer for us." He grinned. "But we make up for it—some of us celebrate twice a year, in December and then again in July. How's that for Christmas spirit?"

Hamadi had been listening to all this with obvious fascination. "I am a Muslim, and do not have Christmas, though Christians in Egypt do celebrate," he said. "For me, this time of year means it is usually close to the time of Eid el-Kbir, which some Muslims know as Eid-ul-Adha. That is when we celebrate the sacrifice of Abraham by creating a great feast. We also are told by Muhammad to give a part of this meat to the poor and hungry so that they might join in the celebration."

"That last bit sounds like a tradition we should all embrace," Annike said, raising her glass to him.

They all continued the discussion for a while, until

eventually the talk turned to the exchanging of gifts. "That reminds me," Nicole said. "I have a little something for everyone."

She hurried into the bedroom and retrieved a shopping bag. It was filled with wrapped gifts—both the ones she'd agonized over for so long for her family and friends and a few smaller trinkets she'd picked up for the others at the party.

"Oh, Nicole!" Melina cried with obvious delight as Nicole handed her a small package. "You should not have!"

Nicole smiled. "Merry Christmas." She handed out larger packages to Luc and Annike and small ones to the others, then watched as Melina eagerly ripped hers open. She held up a key chain shaped like the Eiffel Tower with a wreath hung around its tip.

"It's perfect!" the Greek girl cried with a laugh, adding a few words in her own language that Nicole took to mean "thank you."

"You're welcome. Merry Christmas." Nicole watched as Yelena, Brendan, Hamadi, and Isabel found similar key chains in their own packages. After Mike had given her that Stravinsky key chain earlier in the week, she'd asked him for the location of the store where he'd bought it. It had been near one of their filming spots the next day, so she'd gone there during their lunch break and picked up a few of the holiday-themed key chains, thinking they would make good gift toppers for her friends and family. But that morning she'd decided to give them to her guests instead. She'd really wanted to exchange gifts with Annike and Luc on Christmas Day but hadn't wanted the others to feel completely left out.

"Go on—open yours next," Annike urged Luc, who had been watching the others with his larger gift on his lap.

"*Mais bien sûr.* But I suspect I know what it is." He winked at Nicole. She smiled back and didn't deny it—after all, he had helped her choose what she was getting for Annike and Patrice; he clearly suspected she'd chosen something similar for him.

And he was right. His package revealed a handsome leather picture frame. It held a large photo of the two of them dancing at that salsa club on Nicole's second night back in Paris. Nicole hadn't realized at the time that Annike had dug out Nicole's camera to snap that photo, but once she'd seen it on the memory card, she was very glad she had. It was a fantastic picture. She and Luc were in the midst of a crowd of other dancers, but they were in perfect focus, gazing at each other and smiling as they danced.

Nicole hadn't been sure what Luc would think of it. She'd considered substituting a photo of the two of them at the restaurant where they'd gone that first night instead—that one gave off more of a friends-only vibe. But the dancing picture was so good that she hadn't been able to resist.

"Merci mille fois." Luc got up, walked over, and planted a kiss on her forehead. "It is perfect. Now I shall be able to look upon your beautiful face whenever I wish. *Merci.*"

Nicole realized she'd held her breath as he'd approached her. *"De rien,"* she replied. Then she turned to Annike. "Go on—your turn."

Annike's gift was a framed photo as well. For hers, Nicole had found a gorgeous carved wooden frame with spaces for several photos. She'd used not only a couple of pictures she'd taken that week, but also some from their semester in Paris the previous year, including one taken on the beach in the south of France, where they'd gone with some friends one weekend.

"Aj, tack så mycket!" Annike gasped. "Where did you get these?"

"Ada sent them to me through e-mail." Nicole smiled at the thought of their happy-go-lucky Australian friend. "She says Happy Christmas, by the way."

"It is perfect!" Annike jumped up and ran over to give Nicole a hug. "Thank you so much!"

Next it was Nicole's turn to open Annike's gift, a beautiful set of French Christmas ornaments. As she thanked and hugged Annike, Luc had grabbed Annike's photo montage and was peering at it.

"Je le trouve bien," he commented with a playful smirk. "I especially am drooling over this one of you laughing,

Annike. I do not know which impresses me more—Nicole's wonderful photography skills or your own beautiful face, which was destined for the camera."

Nicole just smiled and rolled her eyes. Leave it to Luc to flatter and flirt with them both in one sentence! But she couldn't help feeling comfortable and happy as she sat there watching her friends—old and new—enjoy the festive day and the gifts she'd chosen for them. She knew Patrice would be equally pleased with the photo she'd chosen of the two of them in Venice, which she'd mounted in a pretty silver frame and shipped off to the U.S. the day before.

Maybe I still don't know what to do about my love life, she thought, sneaking a peek at Luc, who was listening with a smile as Melina started singing a Greek Christmas carol. *But at least it's nice to know I haven't lost my shopping skills!*

"I will see you all for New Year's Eve, *sí*?" Isabel said with a wave as she left the apartment. "Until then, *Feliz Navidad,* everyone."

Brendan hurried out after her. "Right," he called back. "What she said!"

Nicole laughed as she watched them go. Melina had left a few minutes earlier, leaving only Annike, Luc, and Yelena still in the flat. The Russian girl was in the kitchen

packing up some of the leftover food and preparing to leave while Annike and Luc were looking at something out one of the windows.

Just then Nicole's phone rang. She answered without checking the number, expecting to hear her mother's voice. Instead, to her surprise, it was Mike.

"I just wanted to call and wish you a Merry Christmas," he said. "I hope you had a good day."

"I did," she said, touched that he was still thinking of her even after she'd essentially dumped him. "What about you? Are you having fun with your parents?"

They chatted for a few more minutes, then said good-bye. As Nicole hung up, she found herself once again thinking about how similar and different people could be. In some ways, Mike reminded her of Nate, her ex-boyfriend—being with him had been easy and comfortable in some of the same ways—though in other ways, the two of them couldn't be more different.

Then there was Luc. He was *totally* different from the other two in almost every way. Was that because he was French?

"Nicole! Yelena! Quickly!" Annike called, waving eagerly. "Come to the window—look, there is a parade of little children in their holiday finery! They are following after someone dressed as Père Noël."

Luc was laughing as he stared through the window. "*Oui,* and they are now being chased by Père Fouettard,

Père Noël's ugly companion who punishes naughty children."

By now Yelena had left her packing to step toward the window, looking curious. Shaking off her pensive mood, Nicole hurried over to join Annike and Luc at the window. It was Christmas—a time for fun and celebration. The deep thoughts would just have to wait.

Chapter Thirteen

From: NicLar@email.com

To: PatriceQT@email.com, Larsons9701@email.com, mtlarson@email.com, katy@email.com, jlars@email.com

Subject: Merry Christmas!

Hi all! Sorry 4 the mass email. I promise I'll send u each a real message soon! But I wanted 2 say thanx 4 the Xmas wishes, & I was thinking about & missing all of u 2day!

Happy holidays to all of u—or as they say here, *Joyeux Noël et bonne année!*

Love,

Nicole

Nicole looked up from her laptop when she heard the apartment door open. It was the day after Christmas, and Annike was due back from the airport at any moment.

"Bonjour," Annike sang out as she opened the door. "Anybody home?"

She walked in, followed by a very tall, very good-looking guy with white-blond hair, bright blue eyes, tanned skin, square chin, high forehead, and a deep dimple in his left cheek. He had a backpack slung over one shoulder.

Nicole grinned. Leaving her laptop open on the coffee table, she hurried over. *"Välkommen till Paris!"* she said, using one of the bits of Swedish she'd picked up from Annike. "You must be Berg."

"*Hej.* Indeed, you are correct. And you must be the famous Nicole," Berg replied in a friendly baritone, his entire face relaxing into an easy, open smile. Dropping his bag onto the floor just inside, he stuck out his hand.

Nicole shook it as Annike looked from one to the other of them with a rather giddy smile. "I am so glad you two are finally meeting," she said. "I know you will love each other as much as I love both of you."

"We'll see," Nicole said jokingly. "Berg will have to prove himself to be pretty great for me to think he's worthy of you, Annike."

Luckily, she'd judged Berg's sense of humor correctly. He laughed and snapped to attention, bowing to her. "I shall do my best to live up to those standards, *fröken* Nicole. I swear it."

"Good." Nicole giggled, liking him already. "Then if you give me a minute, I'll clear out and leave you two alone for a while."

"Oh, no!" Annike said immediately. "I thought you could help me show Berg the sights today. He has not visited Paris since he was a boy, and is eager to play the tourist."

"Oui, c'est vrai," Berg said, his French accent nearly as good as Annike's. "Please say you will come with us, Nicole."

Nicole hesitated, trying to guess whether they meant it or not. After a week apart, she'd expected them to want a little alone time together. Were they just being polite in insisting she tag along and help play tour guide?

Then she shrugged. She'd never known Annike to be less than honest with her. And why should she expect Annike's boyfriend to be any less forthcoming?

"Sure," she said with a smile. "That sounds like fun. *Allons-y*!"

The rest of the week between Christmas and New Year's passed quickly. The city was still beautiful with all the lights and decorations of the season, but the streets and businesses were quiet, since so many Parisians had left town to visit relatives in other parts of France. It felt sort of as if Nicole and her friends had the place all to themselves.

Nicole had lots of fun getting to know Berg, who was just as nice and smart and funny as he'd seemed at first meeting. She and Annike took him to all of their favorite places—the museums, the monuments, the gardens and parks, the tiny shops and *le grand magasins*, the S.A.S.S. building and the *métro* and their old *arrondissements*, and various bistros and cafés and miscellaneous little undiscovered corners of the city.

Of course Nicole didn't spend *all* her time with Annike and Berg—after all, she wanted to make sure she gave them *some* romantic couple time in the City of Light! But it had been nice to see Annike so free and happy, not just because Berg was there, but because she had finally told her parents about the TV program. And, just like Annike, when she had been in touch with the talent scout and he tried to convince her to change her mind, she didn't waffle at all!

Most of the rest of the S.A.S.S. gang was staying in Paris through the New Year, and she got together with them a few times. Mike was usually part of the group, but aside from the occasional longing glance, he behaved himself. With each time she saw him, Nicole held out more hope that the two of them really would come out of this with some sort of continuing friendship. And she was glad about that. She had no idea what it was about him—or

perhaps about *her*—that had precluded any chance of romance. But whatever it was, it didn't stop her from caring about him as a friend.

At other times over the course of the week, Nicole found herself wandering on her own through Paris, seeing it through ever more appreciative eyes, knowing that she might not see it again for a while. This was where it had all begun—her new life, her *real* life. She would always be grateful to the city for that.

She would also always be grateful to Luc, who had helped her see his home city's charms. The two of them got together a couple of times for a quick coffee, though Luc was extra busy with work as a result of many of his coworkers at the restaurant being away visiting family. During these brief meetings, Nicole did her best to deflect his usual flirting and keep things friendly but not *too* friendly. After all, she would be leaving Paris for good in just a few days. They seemed to have gotten past that one breathtaking kiss, and she was starting to think that it really had been just one of those extraordinary moments that wasn't meant to be repeated. No matter how she'd felt at the time, she saw no point in complicating things with him now by trying to make it into anything more than that.

Even so, she caught herself thinking about Luc a lot even when he wasn't around. While she was sightseeing with Annike and Berg, any glimpse of the Eiffel Tower brought out a flood of memories. During a conversation with Yelena, Quinn, and Melina about movies and music, she found herself comparing their opinions not only to her own, but also to Luc's. And anytime she witnessed Annike and Berg exchanging a kiss, she would feel her face grow hot as she flashed back to the hungry, searching way Luc had kissed her—and exactly how it had felt to give in and kiss him back the same way.

Still, she supposed that sort of reaction would pass once she left Paris and Luc was relegated once again to being an occasional e-mail correspondent. All she had to do until then was keep reminding herself that there was no point in thinking of him as anything more than that.

"Ready to go?" Annike asked, reaching for her coat, which was slung over the sofa.

"Just about." Nicole bent down to tie her sneakers. "Where did you send Berg off to?"

It was the day before New Year's Eve. Annike and Nicole were preparing to go out shopping in search of silly hats, noisemakers, and other New Year's–themed trinkets.

"He has discovered a hotel where he can watch the *Elitserien*—that is, um, our Swedish league for ice hockey." Annike said. "He is going there to watch the broadcast along with Mike and Brendan and also, I think, Hamadi, who knows nothing of hockey but is curious."

"Boys' day out, huh?" As Nicole finished tying her shoes

and straightened up, her cell phone rang. She glanced at the readout. "Hey, it's Yelena," she said. "Hang on, let me see what she wants—maybe she'll come out and meet us."

One of the advantages of that week's more relaxed schedule was that it had given Nicole the chance to get to know Yelena a little better. Beneath her shy, reserved exterior and tentative English lay a very intelligent person with a good sense of humor and an interesting view of the world. Nicole wished she hadn't spent most of the previous week avoiding the Russian girl because of her proximity to the insufferable Quinn.

"Bonjour," she greeted Yelena. "What are you doing today? Feel like some shopping?"

"Shopping?" Yelena repeated.

In the background, Nicole heard another voice repeat the word, though much louder and with a distinctive British accent. She winced. Obviously, Yelena was with Quinn. Still, it was too late to take back her invitation now. Before she knew it, both Yelena and Quinn were agreeing to meet her and Annike on a certain corner in a nearby shopping district.

She hung up and told Annike what had happened. "Sorry," she said. "It looks like we're stuck with The Mouth today." She grimaced. "It's bad enough we have to put up with her tomorrow night." The entire S.A.S.S. gang—plus Luc and Berg—was planning to get together for New Year's Eve on the Champs-Élysées, where Luc and the other Paris natives had assured them there was a big, open-air public gathering every year.

"It is okay," Annike said. She had never seemed quite as bothered by Quinn as Nicole was anyway, and having Berg around this week had turned her always sunny nature even warmer and kinder, if such a thing was possible. "We shall have fun regardless. Both tomorrow and today. Now come, let us get going before half the day is gone!"

"Oi! Check this out, girls!" Quinn grabbed a felt beret colored like the French flag. She balanced it on her head, made a goofy face, and did a little jig around the store, which earned her a perplexed glance from the shopkeeper. She only made a few steps before the hat slipped off and fell to the floor. "Bloody hell!" she exclaimed loudly.

Nicole laughed along with the others at the British girl's clowning around. Despite her reservations, Quinn wasn't annoying her too much as the four of them browsed through a souvenir shop for appropriate New Year's Eve knickknacks.

Just then Nicole heard her phone ring in her bag. Fishing it out, she saw that it was Luc.

"Allô?" she answered.

"If I did not know better, I would think that was a real Parisian girl on the other end of the line," he said with a laugh. "*Quoi de neuf,* Nicole?"

"Pas grand-chose," she replied. "I'm out shopping with

the girls for stuff for tomorrow night." She added the name of the street they were on.

"What luck! I happen to be just around the corner at the moment," he said. "Perhaps I should join you *pour un moment.* I am always interested in spending time with groups of girls, as you know."

She rolled her eyes and laughed. "Yeah, I know."

"Who is it?" Quinn demanded, poking her in the arm. "Tell 'em you're busy, mate!"

"It's Luc," Nicole said, more for the benefit of Annike, who was looking at her curiously, than in response to Quinn's question. "He's inviting himself along shopping with us."

She hadn't bothered to cover the mouthpiece, and Luc laughed. "Ah, do not make me sound such an oaf!" he said. "I only wish to give you the benefit of my knowledge of Paris. I can show you the best spots to buy anything."

"Luc—ooh, isn't he that dishy French bloke of yours I've heard you talk to Annike about, Nic?" Quinn said loudly. "Let him come! We could use some eye candy, eh, girls?" She elbowed Yelena so hard that the Russian girl let out a startled squeak and then rubbed her side.

On the other end of the phone, Luc was still laughing. "*Oui,* let me come, *chérie,*" he said. "Tell me exactly where you are and I shall be there shortly."

He was as good as his word. Within fifteen minutes he was walking into the shop. As usual, he looked handsome, and as usual, Nicole felt her heart flutter a bit when he sought her out with his eyes and smiled at her. Also as usual, she did her best to ignore that flutter.

"*Salut*, ladies," he greeted them, widening his smile to include all four of them. *"Ça va?"*

Quinn giggled. "Ooh-la-la—why is it that French always sounds so much better coming from a good-looking man?"

"Au contraire," Luc said playfully. "Every language sounds better in the mouth of a beautiful woman."

Nicole rolled her eyes. "Come on, let's move on," she suggested. "That shopkeeper is starting to look at us like he thinks we're going to rob the place or something."

"Oh, I do not think that is why he is staring." Luc smirked and looked her up and down. "I can think of a much more likely reason for a man to behave so when the four of you are before his lucky eyes."

"You are too much, Luc," Annike said with a laugh. "But come, Nicole is right. Time to move on."

They wandered outside and over to the next shop. Nicole couldn't help noticing that Quinn was walking right beside Luc, laughing loudly at everything he said.

Things went much the same way for the next hour or so. Whatever annoyance with Quinn that Nicole had been lacking earlier on built up more and more as the British girl flirted shamelessly with Luc at every opportunity.

Although I suppose I can't totally blame her, she thought

irritably as she watched Quinn rest her hand on Luc's arm for a long moment as they looked at something on a store shelf. *As usual, Luc is perfectly willing to flirt his little French face off with anyone without a Y chromosome.*

She found herself brooding over that a bit as their little group wandered along. Ever since that kiss—and okay, perhaps even before that—she'd been getting herself all worked up over Luc and how she really felt about him. But was she just kidding herself? No matter how attracted to him she might be, there was no guarantee that he felt even close to the same way about her. Maybe she was reading him all wrong; after all, she already knew that flirting came as easily to him as breathing...

She was almost relieved when he finally excused himself. "I am afraid I must go to work now," he said. "But I shall see you all *demain* for the big celebration, *n'est-ce pas?*"

"Oui oui!" Quinn said. "You can count on it."

He smiled, then gave a little wave to all of them. "Until then." On his way past, he paused just long enough to give Nicole a squeeze on the arm. *"À bientôt,"* he added.

Quinn stared after him as he left the store. "I say, Nic. You're a lucky girl to have a choice squeeze like that."

"Luc and I are just friends," Nicole said quickly, doing her best to ignore the tingling on her arm where he'd touched her.

"Get away!" Quinn looked dubious, but then she

shrugged. "If that's true, I suppose he's available. Perhaps I'll have to see if he might want to be more than friends with *me* tomorrow night, eh?" She chortled and nudged Yelena. "I mean, I wouldn't mind being more than friends with *that* for a night or two, if you know what I mean!"

Nicole gritted her teeth but kept quiet as the British girl continued on in the same vein. After all, what could she say? Luc was a big boy—if Quinn wanted to throw herself at him tomorrow night, he would just have to take care of himself.

"Checking e-mail?" Annike peered over Nicole's shoulder.

"Uh-huh. I just sent out some of the photos we took on Christmas to our friends from last year." Nicole glanced up from her laptop. Her friend was combing out her damp hair, wrapped in her robe. It was New Year's Eve, and the two girls had banished Berg from the apartment while they primped and prepared for that evening's festivities.

Realizing that she was behind—she'd taken a shower and dried her hair already but was still dressed in the ratty sweats she'd thrown on afterward—Nicole signed off and closed her computer. Then she stood, stretched, and checked her watch.

"Suppose I'd better get dressed," she said.

Annike followed her into the bedroom. "Are you all right?" she asked with concern. "You do not seem very excited about tonight."

"I guess I'm sort of not." Nicole should have known that Annike would notice that she was feeling moody, even though she'd been doing her best to hide it. "This is going to sound stupid, but I'm still kind of cranky over what Quinn said yesterday—you know, about trying to hook up with Luc tonight." She shrugged. "I know it's ridiculous..."

"Oh, but it is not ridiculous at all!" Annike perched on the edge of the bed as Nicole quickly shed her sweats and started pulling on the outfit she'd picked out for that night. "It is perfectly understandable."

"Really?" Nicole yanked at her top to straighten it. "Because *I* don't understand it at all. Luc and I are just friends, you know that. Why should I care if some girl has the hots for him?" She grimaced. "Not that this particular girl is anywhere near good enough for him..."

Annike gazed at her thoughtfully. "A few days ago, you challenged me as to why I caved in and did something I did not want to do," she said. "I admit it, for a moment when you said it, I was a bit angry. And now I am going to risk making you a bit angry, because I am going to ask you—why are you really so upset if Quinn likes Luc? And do not say you are not. Just ask yourself: Why? Why does it matter so much to you?"

Nicole stared at her, too startled by the question to feel the predicted anger. Why *did* she care so much? Was it because of those confusing feelings that kiss had brought to the surface? Or was she mostly reacting to Quinn's obnoxious behavior? Did her reaction have more to do with Quinn—or with Luc?

"Thank you," she said slowly, still staring at Annike as the turmoil in her head suddenly stilled, showing her the truth that should have been staring her in the face all along. "I think maybe you just helped me decide what to—"

She was cut off by the loud ringer of Annike's phone, which was lying on her bed nearby. "Oops!" Annike dove for it. "Sorry about that. I turned it way up so I could hear if Berg called while I was in the shower." She glanced at it and frowned. "I do not recognize this number... Hello?" she answered.

Nicole could hear a torrent of Russian words coming from the other end. She raised both eyebrows, surprised. "Yelena?" she mouthed.

Annike nodded, looking confused. "*S'il te plaît,* Yelena," she said into the phone. "Remember, I do not understand much Russian..."

She paused and listened. Yelena's voice continued, sounding rushed and panicky. Along with a few confusing English words and more incomprehensible Russian, she kept repeating one French phrase: *"Je suis perdu! Je suis perdu!"*

She's lost? Nicole thought, confused.

Annike said a few words in Russian, then continued in French. She paused to listen—by now Yelena's voice was

quieter and Nicole couldn't hear what she was saying.

Finally Annike covered the mouthpiece. "I am not certain of the details," she said quietly, "but it seems that Quinn insisted on traveling to some suburb—Vincennes, I think?—because her family friends said she must see the castle there."

"So now they're lost?" Nicole asked.

"Not exactly." Annike bit her lip. "Quinn met some cute guy and abandoned Yelena without a backward glance. And Yelena doesn't have enough money to get back on her own!"

Chapter Fourteen

"Hold on a moment," Annike told Yelena. "Nicole and I will figure something out."

"Do you know how to get to Vincennes?" Nicole asked.

Annike shook her head. "I am not certain just where it is," she admitted. "Although I suppose we could figure it out…"

Nicole was already on her feet, hurrying out to the main room for her own phone. She dialed quickly as Annike followed her.

"Luc?" she said when he answered. "It's me. Listen, we

have a problem here." She quickly filled him in on Yelena's dilemma. "Can you help?"

"Pas de problème," he said. "Give Yelena my number—tell her to call me right now and describe exactly where she is. I shall pick you up *en peu de temps*."

Moments later Annike was scribbling a note for Berg, and then she and Nicole headed for the door, planning to wait for Luc downstairs. They didn't have long to wait. Almost as soon as they emerged from the building, they saw him hurrying down the street toward them.

"Thanks for coming," Nicole said, realizing at once how relieved she felt with his arrival and how she could always count on him.

"C'est la moindre des choses," he said, already gesturing for them to follow him to the *métro*. "Now come—let us go and rescue poor Yelena."

By the time they got back to the flat with Yelena, Berg had returned. He looked a bit confused as they all burst in.

"Hej," he greeted them, holding up Annike's note. "What is this about running away to the suburbs?"

Annike laughed and hurried over to give him a kiss. "I shall explain later," she said, then added a few words in Swedish.

Just then there was a knock on the door. Nicole went and opened it to find Mike, Melina, Brendan, Hamadi, and Isabel outside. *"Bonne Année!"* they all cried out in unison.

"Let's party!" Brendan added with a whoop.

"Hang on," Nicole said. "Yelena, do you still feel up to coming with us tonight?"

"What's that?" Brendan exclaimed.

Mike looked confused. "Why wouldn't she come along?"

"Oh, but you must come—what's the matter?" Melina hurried over to Yelena.

Before long the whole story was out. "Oh, I see," Isabel said sympathetically. "Well, I suppose I can understand you might not be in the proper mood for a party after all that."

"But it shall not be the same without you." Hamadi stared at Yelena with wide, sorrowful eyes.

Yelena glanced around at all of them, then laughed. "Oh, please do not look at me so sad!" she exclaimed, her eyes beginning to regain their usual quiet sparkle. "It is true, this day has not been what I am wishing. But why should I let that ruin all the fun?" She clapped her hands and smiled. "Of course I am coming! Let us go have a party for the New Year!"

"Opa!" Melina cheered so enthusiastically that everyone burst out laughing.

"Well said." Luc smiled. "Now you all have heard what Yelena has ordered—it is time to celebrate!"

Before long their little group was joining the crowds already gathering on the Champs-Élysées. It was a wild

and crazy scene. The entire area was packed with people, and the place was a whirlwind of lights, music, dancing, and laughter. At the far end of the avenue, the Arc de Triomphe rose above it all, its massive angles outlined in lights that seemed to reflect the stars twinkling in the cold night sky overhead. Nicole felt the stress that Yelena's "rescue" had brought on melting away as she followed her friends through the chaos.

"Oh, my!" Annike said, sounding rather breathless as she took it all in. *"Il y a du monde ici!"*

"Justement," Luc said. "And now we are here, too, and so the party can truly begin!"

With a smile, he turned to help Nicole step down from a curb, and as she took his hand for a moment her mind returned to her earlier conversation with Annike—and the important decision she'd finally reached. But then he let go, and she saw Brendan, Isabel, and Melina rush past and start dancing nearby. Shrugging off all thoughts of past and future, Nicole smiled and joined in. There would be time to deal with the other stuff later.

For the next hour or so they all had fun as a group. They staked out their own spot on the avenue, dancing in a circle and joking around with one another and with other partiers nearby. At one point Nicole saw Yelena struggling to hear the cell phone pressed to her ear.

"Who was that?" she shouted over the music as the other girl hung up.

"It was Quinn," Yelena called back. "She is calling to see if I find my way home."

Mike, Annike, and Berg were dancing nearby and overheard. "Boo!" Mike shouted, grabbing Yelena by the waist and swinging her around. "Forget her. She doesn't deserve you as a friend."

Yelena giggled, obviously taken aback. Nicole smiled at Mike over the other girl's head, and he winked back at her.

The lights all around made it hard to keep track of the time. Nicole was surprised when she checked her watch after what seemed like only moments to find that it was already a few minutes to midnight. She glanced around to see if the others had noticed. A few yards away, Annike and Berg had separated themselves from the group a bit and seemed to be slow-dancing, gazing into each other's eyes. As Nicole watched, Berg bent down and kissed Annike softly.

Nicole shivered and averted her eyes. Mike, Yelena, and Hamadi had wandered off to watch a street performer a short distance away. Isabel was dancing with a cute French guy from the next group over. Brendan, Luc, and Melina were the only ones still dancing in their original spot.

Hurrying over to them, Nicole tapped Luc on the arm. "Can I talk to you?" she said.

"D'accord." With a quick nod to the others, Luc followed her away.

It wasn't easy to find a private spot in the middle of the enormous outdoor party. But eventually Nicole found a deep doorway off one of the side streets. She grabbed Luc's hand and pulled him up the step to join her there.

"Que puis-je pour toi?" He gazed down at her, his face striped with shifting shadows from the whirling lights nearby. The sounds of the celebration were muffled and he was able to speak in a normal tone of voice. "Alone at last—a most pleasant surprise indeed. But what is so urgent that you must speak to me now, just when it is nearly the midnight hour?"

Nicole smiled up at him. Now that the moment was here, she felt nervous and excited and uncertain, all at the same time.

"I wanted to apologize," she blurted out.

He looked confused. "Apologize, *mon amie*?" he said. "But what do you mean? I already told you, I was happy to help find Yelena earlier."

She shook her head. "No, not that. I wanted to apologize for wasting so much time keeping you at arm's length. I was doing what you always warned me about—overthinking things." Taking a deep breath, she held his gaze steadily. "I tried to deny what I was feeling when I saw you again because my brain kept telling me it wouldn't work—you and me, that is."

"Oh, I see."

She couldn't quite read his voice or expression, so she just plunged on. "Even after that—that kiss, I kept telling myself that there was no future for us, and that I shouldn't ruin our friendship over one kiss."

"*Oui,* that does sound like you." Amusement played over his face, but he didn't say anything else.

She took his hands in hers. "But then I remembered something you said once—*ça s'arrangera,* I think it was."

He shrugged, squeezing her hands. "*Oui,* that sounds like me."

"And, well, I decided you were right." She didn't bother explaining about Mike, or the situation with Quinn, or what Annike had said. None of that mattered right now. The only thing that mattered was making him understand what she was telling him. "Why do I have to figure out what the future holds right now? Nobody can do that anyway, and meanwhile I was wasting time when I could be—well, you know. Experiencing new things." She took another deep breath. "Do you have any idea what I'm saying here?"

"Mais oui." He dropped one of her hands and brushed her cheek with his fingertips. "I do not think anything is being lost in translation, *chérie.*"

She shivered as he tucked a strand of her hair behind her ear. "Good," she whispered. "Um, *je ne sais plus ce que je dis*. But like I said, I'm really sorry. We've wasted so much time over the past week..."

"Passons," he shushed her. "There is no such thing as wasted time, Nicole. There is only the present. All that matters is what you are going to do right now."

Nicole was vaguely aware that, out on the street, people were chanting: "... *trios... deux... un...*"

"It's midnight," she said. Glancing to the side, she realized she could just see the edge of the Arc in the distance. It stood there, shadowy yet substantial, looking as eternal as Paris itself.

A cheer went up from the crowd. But Nicole hardly heard it. Luc had just put both his arms around her and pulled her closer, locking his green eyes on hers so intently that she nearly forgot to breathe.

"*On a le temps pour faire tout,* Nicole, *ma chérie,*" he murmured. *"Je t'adore. Commençons au début."*

The way he was looking at her sent sparks through Nicole's entire body. She slipped her arms around his waist, wondering why she'd waited so long. If only...

But no; she shook that off. Luc was right. The only thing that was important was right now. She could figure out the rest later—as the French said, *Chaque chose en son temps*—each thing in its own time. She had two more days in Paris, and she intended to make the most of them.

Out on the street, the crowds were singing now, and someone had just set off some amateur fireworks nearby. But Nicole hardly heard any of it. All her senses were filled with Luc.

Finally, just when she wasn't sure she could stand it another second, he bent and kissed her. She forgot about past, future, and everything else as she melted into the kiss and just enjoyed being fully in the moment.